This is number **171**
of a Limited Edition of 990
Hardbound Volumes - 1991

Greg Girard

1/92

The Land of Dead Giants

llustrator: Kate "Docky" Ferry

Author and Publisher: Greg "Dancing Bear" Guirard

Layout: Judy "Frankie" Henry

Design: Greg Guirard, Kate Ferry, Judy Henry, Marce Lacouture

Primary Editing Assistant: Marce "Scooter" Lacouture

Additional Editing and Advice:

> Heidi "The Voice" Cunningham
>
> Janice "Janzie" Aillet-Crochet
>
> Bernard E. "The D.A." Boudreaux, Jr.
>
> beren "bear" gaule
>
> Michelle "Mitch" Guirard
>
> Harold Perrin "Andy" Anderson, Jr.
>
> André "Cruteville" Guirard

Typing and Re-Typing (and Re-Typing): Tracey "Faithful Pal" Hirsch

First printing: November 1991

ISBN: Softbound—0-9624778-1-8

> Hardbound—0-9624778-2-6

Typesetting: Holly McGregor Carruth, *Cablecast Magazine*

Cover design by Greg Guirard

The Land of Dead Giants

by
Greg Guirard

Illustrated
by
Kate Ferry

Contents

List of Characters—The Year Is 1948

Aristile "Vieux Pop" Guilbeau—age 78—a Cajun fisherman and thinker, born in the Atchafalaya Basin in 1870.

Alexson "Ti Frere" Shellgrave—age 12—grandson of Aristile, and a student of the old man's teaching.

Octavie Guilbeau Shellgrave—age 38—a woman who was born and raised on Bayou Goujaune, daughter of Aristile and mother of Alexson.

Wilferd "Brother" Shellgrave—age 37 when last seen in 1944—a full-time poacher of wildlife, husband of Octavie and father of Alexson.

Choupique LaCouture—age 28 in 1890—a logger who chooses to defend the largest cypress tree in the swamp.

Eulalie "Big Mom" Guilbeau—age approximately 100—Aristile's mother, who lives in town, plays cards for entertainment, and insists that everyone make a special effort to be happy every day.

Galveston Guilbeau—age 65—son of Eulalie and brother of Aristile, adventurer and world traveler, intent on taking over South America, according to Eulalie.

Lash Larue—age approximately 27—a Hollywood cowboy movie star, born in Louisiana, an amazing talent with a bullwhip.

Crapeau Ardoin—age 76—one of Aristile's old friends, a fisherman who loves to eat, play cards and make music.

Placide "Seed" Laviolette and Clairmille Trosclair—age mid-70's—two old friends of Crapeau and Aristile, members of the regular cooking, card-playing and music-making group.

Wilson—age 35—a logging boss intent on cutting down every cypress tree large enough to produce marketable lumber.

Sherwood Anderson—1876 - 1941—American novelist and short-story writer born in Ohio. For a time in the mid-1920s, Anderson lived in New Orleans, where he met and spent a memorable afternoon with Aristile Guilbeau.

Moccasin—Alexson's mixed-breed dog and constant companion, except when the boy is in school learning to speak English.

Ti Bird—a red-shouldered hawk rescued as a chick and raised by Alexson.

Terms Unfamiliar to Some Readers

(Those readers who know everything already are welcome to skip this part.)

bayou—a small natural stream with slow-moving water, except in times of flood. From the Choctaw *bayuk* for creek or small river. A bayou can flow through a swamp as well as through drier areas.

swamp—a natural low-lying area, usually covered by water, where plant growth is generally limited to baldcypress, water tupelo and small shrubs which can tolerate year-round inundation. Aquatic plants, such as water hyacinth and duck weed dominate the surface.

marsh—a low, watery area with few trees, usually closer than a swamp to a body of salt water, such as the Gulf of Mexico, where various shrubs and grasses flourish, some with a high tolerance for salt or brackish water.

levee—a long, raised earthen structure, a dike, generally built to guide or control the flow of water. There is a levee bordering the eastern and western sides of the Atchafalaya Basin, built by the Corps of Engineers in the early 1930s.

Atchafalaya—"the deepest river in the world," a relatively short river running south from mid-Louisiana into the Gulf of Mexico. From the Choctaw *hacha falaya* for "long river." The Atchafalaya receives most of its water, and silt, from the Mississippi River.

baldcypress—the most common tree in the swamp, an extremely valuable tree for its wood, which is durable, easily worked and resistant to termites and rot.

pirogue—a small, flat-bottomed, canoe-like boat, formerly made of cypress, now usually made of marine plywood, fiberglass or aluminum, powered by a paddle and commonly used before the time of outboard motors for fishing, moss-gathering and travel.

trading boat—a large, wooden, flat-bottomed river boat usually belonging to a fish buyer located in a city or town. Trading boats would visit fishermen living along the Atchafalaya River every two or three days. Fishermen held their catch in "liveboxes" (framed enclosures of chicken wire which were partially submerged in the river or bayou and in which fish were kept, awaiting transfer to the hold of a trading boat). Swamp and river dwellers generally traded their fish for clothing, fuel, hardware, canned goods, fresh meat, ice, or whatever they might order and have delivered on the trading boat's next trip into their area.

Children who gave trouble might have to face such graphic threats as: "If you don't behave, I'm gonna hold you in the livebox and trade you for a can of green beans when the next boat comes."

crosscut saw—a six to eight-foot-long handsaw operated by two men, one on a handle at each end, and used to cut down cypress and other marketable trees in the basin of the Atchafalaya River and elsewhere.

springboard—a stout piece of lumber six feet long with a metal "lip" bolted to one end. Holes five to six inches deep were chopped into a tree trunk, and a springboard was jammed into each hole, providing the logger with a narrow, horizontal platform on which to stand while using his axes or crosscut saws.

annual rings—growth rings of a tree which are revealed and can be counted when the trunk is cut through and the tree falls away. Each ring usually represents one year's growth, so it is easy to determine a tree's age by counting them.

alligator gar—a large, edible freshwater fish once abundant in the swamps and rivers, and frequently weighing over two hundred pounds.

gaspergou or goo—a local name for an edible scale fish more commonly known elsewhere as freshwater drum.

goujaune—the yellow catfish, a favorite for eating among the Cajun fishermen themselves.

choupique—a bowfin, a swamp fish considered bony and unappetizing by some, but prized by others. Choupique breathe air and survive dry periods by burrowing into the wet mud of bayou or lake bottoms.

buffalofish or buffalo—another river and bayou fish of commercial value, a *sac-a-lait*—the white perch or crappie. A panfish highly prized for sport and eating.

en Ville—in New Orleans, a Cajun name for Louisiana's biggest city.

Chitimacha Indians—a tribe of native Americans who lived, fished and hunted in the lower Atchafalaya Basin area before the white people arrived. The Chitimacha live today in the small town of Charenton, on the lower western side of the Basin.

muscadines—wild grapes that grow on vines in the big oaks along the bayou. Muscadines are used in making jelly and wine.

grosbec—the yellow-crowned night heron, now protected by federal game laws, but frequently eaten by Cajuns anyway.

hoopnet—a cylindrical mesh net from three to six feet in diameter and seven to twelve feet long, whose shape is maintained by a series of bent wood, steel or fiberglass hoops.

crapeau—a frog or toad.

Cajun French—a 17th century form of the language based on common usage rather than on a dictionary or a written form. When the Acadians arrived in Louisiana in the mid-1700s, their language began to receive additions and other changes from the Spanish, the Indians, and the black Africans, as well as from English. Extensive variations in the Cajun French language can frequently exist between one area in Cajun country and another, sometimes even between neighboring communities.

for Hannah - 3/3/91

The author wishes to acknowledge, with considerable gratitude, the financial assistance provided by the following individuals and/or companies toward the publication of this book:

Ken & Amy Burns - Florentine Films; Walpole, New Hampshire
C. Paul Hilliard - Badger Oil Company; Lafayette, Louisiana
John and Joretta Chance - Lafayette, Louisiana

Prologue

The Atchafalaya Basin is a vast area of nearly one million acres of forests, bayous, swamps, rivers, and lakes. For two centuries it was home for several thousand fishermen, hunters, loggers, trappers and their families. Now the logging has ended, since all of the big trees were felled and cut into lumber many years ago. Almost all the fishermen have moved their homes to communities bordering the eastern or western edges of the Basin, outside the big levees that contain and define it. Because the fishing grounds are still productive, hundreds of fishermen enter the Basin in outboard rigs on a daily basis and leave at day's end with their catch of crawfish, catfish and other finfish, turtles and frogs. They have moved from the Basin itself to avoid the spring flooding that occurs there regularly and because they have become accustomed to having the conveniences of modern life close at hand: supermarkets, schools, jobs, television, telephones, automobiles and shopping malls. They have given up a great deal to gain little.

For the most part, this story does not concern the people who left the swamps. It deals instead with an older way of life—that of a people who lived close to the big woods and the waters, who lived from day to day on the fish they could catch and the birds and animals they could hunt. Though they would sometimes sell their catch to the trading boat companies for money, they more frequently exchanged their fish for other food, for clothing, fuel, shotgun shells, or tools. There was little need for currency except on rare trips to the little towns on the edges of the great Basin, where they could purchase articles not readily available on the trading boats.

Their houses were simple and well constructed, and their yards usually contained an assortment of domestic animals such as a milk cow, chickens, ducks, and geese, and a family of hogs.

Like most people in South Louisiana in those brave simple days, they spoke Cajun French and very little English. To be sure, there were communities here and there in the Basin where English predominated. After the American Civil War, many homeless and jobless people moved into South Louisiana where they could find work in the lumber industry, and where fish and wildlife were still abundant. These people came from several states, including Mississippi, Alabama and Tennessee, and they were speakers of English. But the individuals whose lives are a part of the story you are about to read—Aristile Guilbeau and his little family—were Cajuns, and they spoke Cajun French.

To simplify matters for those of you who never learned to read or speak Cajun French or Cajun English, the dialogue is written in standard English, reducing its flavor considerably, like a sauce picante without cayenne pepper, but making it intelligible. Life is a tradeoff, and compromises must be made at every turn, it seems. Only on rare occasions when Aristile tries to say something in English are his words written as he really says them: "Not'ing lasses fuh evah," as he used to say, and even Cajun French has had its day.

It would be unfortunate, however, if the reader were unable to fix in his mind the pronunciation of at least three French words—*vieux, frere,* and *'ti'*. *Ti* is easy enough, and for convenience I have dropped the apostrophes: say Tee, which means little, and comes from *petit. Vieux* means old, and is pronounced almost like view, but instead of a "u" sound at the end, substitute the first half-syllable of the word earth or early. *Frere* means brother, and it rhymes with where, but roll the first "r." Try it a few times.

If you can't get it right, call me. I live on the outside edge of the Basin too, and I have a telephone.

The Land of Dead Giants

Big Mom told my mama once that she likes my dad better now that he's dead. That's one of the things she thinks about every day to make her happy. "You know, Baby Girl," she said to Mama, "I like ol' Wilferd just fine now that he's dead. But let me tell you right now, he better stay that way if he knows what's good for him." Mama didn't say anything. She looked at me where I sat at Big Mom's dining table, eating blackberry pie, but I couldn't tell if she was sad or embarrassed or angry. She never wants to talk to me about my dad. I can look right at her and say, "Mama, is my dad coming back someday?" or "Why didn't my dad take me out in the woods with him like Vieux Pop does?" or "Did my dad like me?" And she'll just say, "Eat your gumbo before it gets cold, Ti Frere," or "Don't forget to milk the cow before dark," as if I never asked her anything at all.

Names

Almost every Cajun boy in those days had a nickname that generally stayed with him for his entire life. Ti Frere had a given name, Alexson, but most people called him Ti Frere anyway because that was the custom. How did he get the name Ti Frere? Simple. His father, Wilferd, was born the last of six brothers and five sisters, and the baby's parents were at a loss to come up with one more name, so they put off formal naming until the boy was almost two years old, at which time they chose the name Wilferd, having heard the name Wil*fred* once or twice on their old radio. But they had begun calling him "Brother" from the beginning, for lack of a formal name. Wilferd was not Cajun and could not speak French, but when he and Octavie had a son, the boy became known as Ti Frere (Little Brother) anyway, since the Guilbeau family was distinctly Cajun.

On a bitterly cold and rainy night one January, when Alexson was eight years old, Wilferd had failed to return from a poaching trip in the Basin, and his body was never found.

Aristile had been called "Steel" as a young man, then Pop by his children and eventually Vieux Pop by his grandson Ti Frere, to distinguish him from Pop, which is what Ti Frere called his father. Only Aristile and Octavie called Wilferd Wilferd. Others called him Brother, or Brudda.

Ti Frere would continue to be called Ti Frere if he stayed relatively small or short. Otherwise he would gradually come to be called simply Frere. But for the time being Ti Frere remained Ti Frere, and Vieux Pop remained Vieux Pop.

These people, excepting Wilferd, grew up speaking Cajun French, and they learned and accepted English reluctantly, as it was the language of outsiders to them, the language of big landowners from other states, oil men from Texas and Oklahoma and voices on the radio. Aristile spoke almost no English at all until he was middle-aged, and he always felt more comfortable expressing himself in Cajun French. It was a matter of considerable satisfaction to him that Ti Frere also preferred that language.

Like all the children his age, Alexson was forced by threat of punishment to learn and always speak English at school, but he usually spoke only Cajun French when he was away from school.

The home of Aristile, Octavie and Alexson was a one-story unpainted cypress structure surrounded by a picket fence made of hand-split cypress. There was a front porch across the entire width of the house and

a back porch as well. The big yard contained several other buildings: a chicken coop, three dog houses with pens, a small barn for the milk cow and the hogs, an outhouse, a shed for tools and storage area for dry firewood. In a separate fenced area was a sizeable vegetable garden. There were pear and fig trees and a small citrus orchard, and there was a small field where Aristile grew corn to feed the animals and also sweet potatoes, melons and whatever else suited his fancy. There were several rose bushes. Everything grew well in the rich soil of the river delta.

There was a tar vat with a wooden structure above it that allowed Aristile, by using ropes and a pulley, to dip his hoopnets into hot tar periodically in order to preserve them from rotting. The house itself was no more than twenty feet from the bank of Bayou Goujaune, so named because it contained an abundance of yellow catfish.

The Guilbeaus had lived in the Atchafalaya Basin for several generations. Almost from the beginning of the Acadian relocation from eastern Canada to Louisiana in the 1760s, the Guilbeau family was known to have a love for unspoiled nature and the big woods in their blood. Aristile's father was recognized as one of the best fishermen and hunters in the entire Basin. He dropped dead of heart failure one day while pulling a heavily-loaded hoopnet into his boat. He was ninety years old, and the fisherman who found him claimed that the old man still had a smile on his face.

Aristile's wife and four-year-old son had died years earlier when fire consumed the houseboat on which the family was living during that spring's flood. Octavie, who was ten at the time, was spared only because she had begged to accompany her father early that day when he left to raise his nets, and he had agreed.

Wilferd

Wilferd was proud of his marksmanship: "I seen the day when a pair of wood ducks was comin' straight over me, almost dark, and I had my ol' single-shot 12-gauge; used to hold one shell in my left hand against the front stock, so I could reload real quick. Well, I dropped the first duck right at my feet, reloaded without takin' my eyes off the second one, and dropped that one too, as it was goin' away from me. Now that was quick— two woodies with a single-shot Remin'ton. Tell you one thing: I don't mess around when it comes to killin' ducks."

One thing Wilferd didn't tell about was the time he had tested his new deer rifle on some beavers that had a lodge a hundred yards or so from a little camp he had on the edge of Buffalo Swamp where he did most of his poaching. Wilferd shot two of them and left them there to rot, didn't even skin them for the pelts, because there wasn't enough easy money in it. A few weeks later, when he was away, the other beavers came by and cut down the biggest tree growing close to his camp—a black willow about 2 1/2 feet in diameter—and made it fall right on the shack. Smashed it to

pieces. Wilferd used that as an excuse to shoot beavers whenever he saw them, but he never rebuilt his poaching camp, and it was the following winter that he disappeared.

Ti Frere was his son, and Wilferd wanted the boy to grow to be a man like himself, skillful in the woods and swamps, able to find and slaughter wildlife at will, and never, never get caught by the game agents. Wilferd resented all laws that applied in any way to him or his activities. Whenever he could do it safely, he stole from other fishermen and hunters, even those he had known all his life. He took nets and traps, fish, shotguns, paddles, whatever he could pick up and carry off.

Wilferd hated the game agents and the sheriff's deputies whose job it was to prevent theft and poaching, and he gloated over his talent for evading the laws. He would complain loudly, whenever he encountered an agent or deputy, that some crook had stolen his pirogue or his nets.

"Why don't you clowns catch those thieves?" he would yell. "You get a big paycheck and the fastest boats, but you can't even protect the poor people!" It was not true that anyone had stolen from him, and it was not true that lawmen were well paid, but Wilferd liked to say those things anyway.

"Tell you one thing," Wilferd would always begin. Then he'd tell you several things you really didn't want to know, things that were mostly lies anyway, or rumors, or big, unrealistic plans.

Wilferd had his own theory to explain every event and his own analysis of every action. In his eyes, everyone was trying to keep him down or take advantage of him in one way or another.

Years earlier, when Octavie was ready to accept Wilferd's proposal to marry him, she had gone to Aristile for his approval. It was a formality, for she had already decided she would marry Wilferd.

"All vines and no muscadines," he said. Aristile was nothing if not honest and straightforward. He looked Octavie in the eyes and said it again: "All vines and no muscadines."

"But, Pop," Octavie said, "Wilferd's a smart one, and he has plans of all kinds to make us a better life and lots of money. Good plans," she insisted.

"Thunder don't wet the ground," Vieux Pop said, and he was through giving advice that was not wanted.

Pop doesn't like Wilferd, because he's different from most of the young men around here. He can see that there's more to life than setting nets and crawfish traps, hoping that the catch is good enough and the price is fair enough to make a few dollars, working all the time, barely getting by. The buyers will never be fair with the fishermen—everybody knows that, so what's the use?

Big Mom doesn't like Wilferd either, but there's a reason for that. She's getting too old to understand what's going on; and besides, she has a grudge against the whole Shellgrave family. I don't want to live here forever. It's too lonely since Mama died. It's too far away from everything—no friends, no dances, no nothing. Mass on Sunday at the big Catholic church in town, a movie trip now and then, holiday meals at Big Mom's—it's not enough.

Pop would've been happy if I'd married Valsin, but after he drowned trying to save those kids when the trading boat sank in the river, no man would even look at me, out of respect for the memory of Val. What a life I'm having!

An Encounter

One day in April Wilferd had come out of the swamp with his pirogue loaded almost full of young night herons that he had killed when they were nearly big enough to fly out of their nests. The people to whom he sold game were particularly fond of the taste of these tender young birds, and they paid Wilferd a high price for them.

Aristile was just going into the swamp to bait his crawfish traps that day, and he stopped to examine the pirogue loaded with dead birds. It was not his style to criticize the ways of others, but this disgusted him. He always spoke English to Wilferd, by necessity:

"You total-loss dose poor grosbecs, din't you Wilferd? Why you do dat kind of 'ting? You got no right to kill dose helpless yong heron. Why you don' work like any man? If you don' like to fish for a living, you could get you a good job in town, or with one of dose oil company."

"Get out of my way, Aristile," Wilferd shouted. He always called Vieux Pop by his real name. "Don't try to tell me how you think I should live my life." He bumped his father-in-law's pirogue with his own.

Vieux Pop almost never got angry, but he was getting there now. "If you don' stop dis kind of 'ting, Ah'm gonna have to turn you in to de gameward. Ah don' see no udder way to stop you."

"You turn me in, and I'll leave here with your daughter and grandson the same day," Wilferd snarled, "and you'll never see them again, I promise you dat," he said, mocking Aristile's accent. Then he moved on.

Hell, I can make more money in one mornin' than that old fart makes in a week of hard work baitin' and runnin' crawfish traps. And he thinks he can tell me what to do! Before I know it he'll have my kid thinkin' the way he does: "Come here, Ti Frere; let me show you how to patch a pirogue"... "Come with me for a walk, Ti Frere; I want to explain something to you about this and that"...Big deal! Far as I'm concerned, he's just like that old car rotting away out in the swamp, the car on that poster me and Octavie brought him from New Orleans. He keeps it up on his wall like if it was a religious relic or somethin'. I'm gonna use it to start a fire in the woodstove one day—see what he thinks about that.

Aristile paddled on, never looking back at Wilferd and his boatload of dead birds, and his thoughts drifted to his grandson.

Aristile loved Alexson more than anything or anyone, and he had been teaching the boy everything he knew and felt about life in the big woods and the swamps. He didn't think that Ti Frere knew yet of the illegal things his father did, but he suspected that it would not be long before Wilferd began trying to get his son to help him in his shady activities. And Vieux Pop was not certain that his own teachings would stand up to the heavy pressure that he knew Wilferd would use on the young boy.

It was not with deep and genuine sorrow that most people in the area greeted the news of Wilferd's disappearance the following January. Even Aristile, the kindest and most decent man on the bayous, had to admit to himself that he felt more relief than sorrow. It made him sad to see Ti Frere and Octavie so grieved, but he knew that they would all have a better and more peaceful life, now that Wilferd was gone.

There was no funeral, since the search for Wilferd's body had been unsuccessful and was abandoned after several days of combing the swamps and dragging the bayous and the big river, but the family was in formal mourning for several weeks, as was the custom. Aristile was left with an uneasy feeling that Wilferd was not dead at all, but that he had gone into hiding for reasons known only to himself.

That man is too smart and too mean to let the swamp or the river get him, or even a bear or a panther. It's a sad thing to say, even to myself, but I hope I'm wrong to think that he may be in hiding somewhere. I hope I never have to see him again, dead or alive.

Philosophy

Aristile had built his own pirogue, and it didn't have a single splinter, and not one rotten piece of wood anywhere either, even where you couldn't see—the integrity of unseen parts. Sometimes, it seemed to Ti Frere, Vieux Pop lived to do things right, and he found contentment there: "Listen," he would tell the boy, "if you build a set of shelves for the kitchen and you leave a rough place in the wood, or a rotten place or a crack, that's not right, even if the bad piece is against the wall on the bottom side of the shelf and you cover it with a 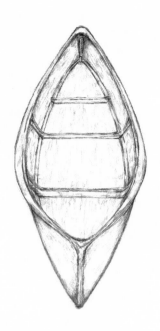 finishing strip and you paint the whole thing and you put the shelves in a cupboard or a closet where it's dark, it's still no good. Every time you go in there and get something off the shelf, you'll remember that rotten place and you'll feel bad about it."

No one could accuse Vieux Pop of being proud or vain in any way, for genuine humility was as much his essence as a dark and mysterious beauty is the essence of the great swamps. But he never regretted being born a Cajun, and he was always grateful for whatever powers had placed him in the Atchafalaya Basin at birth, for he loved every bayou and swamp, every tree and stump and every animal and fish, including those he hunted and killed to feed his family.

It was Vieux Pop who taught Ti Frere to fish and hunt and to let humility guide him rather than pride. "The time will come when you are a better hunter than I am, Ti Frere; and when you kill a beautiful buck so that we can eat, you will feel an excitement unlike any other. Blood will rush to your face, and your heart will pound as if it wants to burst out of your chest. This is good, and as it should be. But you must respect the animal whose life you have taken. There is no denying that the hunt is fun and exciting, but it is wrong to kill only for fun. Never kill more than we can eat, and never lose sight of the possibility that there are spirits everywhere— in the woods and waters, in the air and in the birds and animals and trees themselves, as there are in us. If any life is sacred, then every life is sacred, and it's love for life itself that really matters. You must not ignore or forget that."

Vieux Pop realized that he was preaching, and he almost never did such things. He knew that Ti Frere's understanding of what he had said was limited, but the boy was more than willing to listen. Aristile felt that the words he had spoken would be remembered, and that Alexson would grow to understand them gradually, as the years went by and his experiences accumulated.

Fishing

Almost every Cajun boy, by the age of nine or ten, had begun fishing commercially on a small scale, learning early the skills that would support him and his family as he grew older, if he chose to continue living in or near the Basin.

Ti Frere had his favorite methods of fishing, and one was with floating gar lines. He used the man-sized cast net that his mother had handmade for him to catch bait fish. He would collect ten or twelve dry

willow branches or stakes whose bark had been eaten away by beavers or nutria. To each he would attach a stout cord of three or four feet and to the cord he would tie a steel leader made of old piano wire, for the teeth of an alligator gar can easily cut any rope or string. Then he would put a large hook at the end of the wire and bait it with one or more of the small fish he had caught in the cast net. He would paddle to the middle of the river and place his lines in the water all around his pirogue, then drift downriver, hoping for a large gar to swallow one of his bait fish and pull the stick under water.

I know why Vieux Pop made my pirogue so big. He says he did it that way because a fourteen-footer can carry more fish and I'm getting to be a good fisherman. But I think it's really because he's worried about me being by myself on this deep river. Small pirogues are too easy to turn over. It's all old red cypress from one of the big trees like those whose stumps I see all over the swamp when I run my catfish lines and turtle traps. "Dat ol' oily cypress won' nevah rot, no. You can paddle you to mah funeral in dat same pirogue, Ti Frere. Hit's de bess wood dey got."...Why do people have to get old and die? If God can do things any way He wants, why doesn't He let people get to a certain age and just stay there? I don't want Vieux Pop to ever die.

As he floated with the current, Ti Frere spent his time daydreaming, reading one of his favorite books or practicing English by talking the strange language to himself. Every few minutes he would count his floating stakes. If one or more were missing, he knew that he had hooked a gar or a catfish. Whatever fish he caught would be big because the river was 150 feet deep, and smaller fish stayed mostly near the banks or in the swamps. At least, that was his theory, and he had caught some beautiful fish.

An alligator gar cannot breathe for long under water and must frequently return to the surface for air. Even a catfish, which does breathe when submerged, feels the upward pull of a light wooden stake. It was when the hooked fish returned to the surface that Ti Frere could spot the floating stake and chase it down in order to pull in the catch. It was an exciting moment for the boy when he saw one of his stakes moving across the surface of the river and allowed himself to imagine what fish might be pulling it.

Aristile had once caught a 260-pound garfish in one of his nets and sold it for twenty-three dollars to the fish buyer in town. It was hard enough for Ti Frere to handle a twenty or thirty-pound fish and get it into his pirogue without overturning in the big river, but he dreamed of catching a real "monster" like Vieux Pop's fish. Whatever fish he caught Vieux Pop would sell in town and Ti Frere could use the money to buy shoes or books, more fishhooks or lines, or enough cord for his mother to make him a small hoopnet.

The Woodpecker Tree

Ti Frere loved to explore the swamps on foot or in his pirogue, depending on the season of the year and the depth of the water. He liked best going into remote places where he told himself that no other person, not even Aristile, had ever been. He would hide at the base of one of the the tall hollow cypress trees that had been long dead but was still hard and solid, and a favorite tree for the big pileated woodpeckers that lived in the swamp. And he would wait.

When the bird began to pound loudly with its powerful beak on the upper part of the old tree, Ti Frere would lean his forehead against the trunk so that he could feel the vibrations running through the dense wood and into his own body. Sometimes he would put a hand and a knee against the tree trunk. If the woodpecker were a big one and the tree were tall, though it was only the shell of the tree, he could feel the vibrations in the ground he stood on, and even in the air.

It was at these times, when he stood alone at the woodpecker tree, that Ti Frere felt most in touch with something mystical and mysterious. There was an unexplainable warmth, a sense of significance far beyond his comprehension.

He would carry this feeling with him through the day and into the night so strongly that he would awaken sometimes to a drumming in the air that he recognized as the feeling of the "woodpecker tree." It was always a good feeling, and he would fall asleep again with a smile on his face. Many years later, and hundreds of miles away from the swamp, he would awaken to that same drumming, and at first he would think himself back in his little bed at Vieux Pop's cabin on Bayou Goujaune.

The Town

There were some uncommon people living in the Atchafalaya Basin back in the 1940s, and Aristile Guilbeau was singular among them. He was a widower, and he grew several varieties of roses to honor the memory of his wife, who had loved roses and taught him to love them. He was always giving away roses. Aristile was strong and healthy, honest, sensitive and understanding, generous, gentle and insightful. He was as Cajun as squirrel jambalaya and alligator sauce picante, and he spoke two languages—French and English—though the standard form of either was not nearly as familiar to him as the depths of the great swamps that surrounded his little cypress house on the bayou.

Aristile was born in the Basin, and though he traveled to New Orleans once, he almost never left the swamps and the bayous except on those Saturday evenings when he would take Ti Frere and Octavie to the picture show, as movies were called in those days before television, in the small town just outside the western edge of the Basin. Octavie would sometimes skip the picture show to visit friends in town. The small family would make the four-mile trip in Vieux Pop's putt-putt fishing boat, and if it were a Tarzan film with Johnny Weismuller, Aristile would go into the old theatre on Main Street and see it himself, because he admired Johnny Weismuller for his great abilities as a swimmer and diver. Otherwise he would visit his mother, Eulalie, and hear of the exploits of his brother Galveston Guilbeau, who, according to Eulalie, would soon own all or most of South America. It was Ti Frere's opinion that his Great Uncle Galveston probably led a far more exciting life than anyone else he knew personally.

"Which countries has he been taking over?" I ask Big Mom.

"Countries? They have countries down there, Alec?" At least she knows it's somewhere south of the Gulf of Mexico.

"Well sure, Big Mom, there's plenty countries in South America, and in Central America, too." I've been studying Latin American geography in

school, and I'm showing off.

"There's Argentina and Brazil and Bolivia and Peru and several others. And in Central America there's Guatemala and Honduras, Costa Rica and El Salvador." I can't remember any others.

To her Central and South America are pretty much the same place—"the Tropics." She wouldn't have any interest in the area at all except that my Great Uncle Galveston is somewhere down there, taking control. Vieux Pop says that when Uncle Gal comes back, it'll probably be in a wooden box.

Big Mom had read once, in Reader's Digest probably, that everyone needs to make a special effort to be happy every day. She was stuck on the idea. "Did you remember to be happy today, Alec?" she'd ask me. It would always make me sad.

The only cowboy film Aristile would watch was a Lash Larue picture. Not only was Lash Larue a Louisiana man, but his skill with a bullwhip was amazing as well as authentic. Any clown could ride a horse and beat up bad guys on film, but Lash Larue could do things with a long whip that no one else could, on or off the screen.

He had come to the little town, in person, one Saturday night and performed on stage at the theatre. Aristile himself had gotten involved in a small way. He was sitting up front and had bought a bottled soda for Ti Frere. Just as he was about to open it by pushing up with both thumbs under the edge of the cap, Lash Larue  called out, "Sir, if you will allow me, I'll open that pop bottle for you." So Aristile walked toward the stage, without embarrassment, intending to hand the bottle to Lash Larue, who stood quietly at the left, in the solid black cowboy clothes he always wore. As Aristile began to cross the wide stage from the right, Lash Larue signaled him to stop. "Hold the bottle toward me," he commanded, and Aristile did. In a movement so quick that many in the theatre didn't see it coming, the cowboy in black popped the cap off the bottle with his whip and caught it as it flew toward him. Aristile walked over and shook hands. *"Bien fait,"* Vieux Pop said, "Well done." Then he returned to his seat next to Ti Frere, who was bouncing with excitement and smiling happily.

Lash Larue then had a beautiful young woman assistant stand at a distance of twenty or twenty-five feet from him and hold a burning cigarette between her lips, her profile to him. First he flicked the ash off, slowly and carefully, as though he were not quite sure he could do it safely, taking a long time to aim his whip, so as not to injure the woman's face. Everyone assumed that the trick was over and began to applaud. The young woman did not smile and bow but remained as motionless as a great blue heron waiting for a minnow to surface in the water below it. Then, as quick and unexpected as a bolt of lightning, Lash Larue struck again and again. His big black whip was a blur as it cracked loudly and cut off a small portion of cigarette each time until there was only a tiny length of it extending a fraction of an inch past the woman's lips. The stage around the woman was littered with half-inch fragments of the cigarette.

Lash then bowed and looked at Aristile, who smiled and nodded, then shook his head in disbelief. The audience was so shocked by the loudness and suddenness of what they had just seen that their applause was delayed. After the performance, the film began, and Aristile decided he would like to invite the great Lash Larue to visit and have a meal with him at home, for he admired his talent and wished to know whether his character was equal. When he looked for the cowboy in black, though, he was told that Lash Larue had already left for the next small town, where he was scheduled to perform again later that night.

Ti Frere didn't know that his grandfather had once been nearly as skillful and amazing in his own way, with his own tools, as Lash Larue was now with his bullwhip. That was part of Aristile's dark secret; and if there was an ounce of fear in the nearly fearless old man, it was that Ti Frere would discover his secret before he found the strength to tell the boy about it himself.

When the film was over, Aristile and Alexson walked the few blocks to Big Mom's house, where it had been agreed that they would meet Octavie and have a cup of coffee and a slice of pie before starting for home on the dark bayou that ran by the little town.

Big Mom lives alone in a little house in town. She must be 150 years old. We stop in to see her whenever we go to the picture show, or to Sunday mass. She comes out to our house sometimes for Easter and Christmas, or we go to her place to celebrate holidays and birthdays.

She never cared much for the swamp. It's too wet and stinky, full of alligators and snakes and furry things under logs. She has her friends, and they take turns playing cards at one another's houses. Her name is Eulalie, but it was a surprise to me one day to hear her called that. To me she had always been Big Mom. I said her name over and over until it sounded silly and strange: Eulalie, Eulalie, Eulalie. Sounds, eh? You can repeat them and change them any way you want; you can play with them in your head. And you can do it while you're doing something else, like walking in the woods, or fishing, or painting your pirogue.

A Game of Cards

By the time he was twelve, Ti Frere had heard hundreds of stories about how beautiful and wild the cypress swamps had been in the old days, how there were deer and ducks, black bear, panthers and wildcats, huge fish and snapping turtles, snakes and alligators everywhere. And there were towering cypress trees in every direction, further than the eye could see and even further than a strong man could paddle his pirogue in a week. It was the thought of the dark forest of big trees that always captured his imagination in those days. The boy would often sit on the firewood box in the corner of their cabin and listen to Vieux Pop and his

buddies talk about the old times, while they ate an evening meal of courtbouillon or fried catfish, and then played bourré, their favorite card game, on the kitchen table. On long winter evenings they often played music as well.

If he closed his eyes while they spoke, he could see the great forest of tall straight trees, full of birds and squirrels and raccoons in their branches, deer walking in the shallow water at their bases and black panthers lurking silently in the shadows. There were fish swimming lazily in the clear swamp water and flock after flock of ducks and geese in the sky, calling as they migrated or looked for a place to land and feed.

In the warm little room, with the air scented by wood smoke from the old cookstove, and by the aroma of fresh coffee that his grandfather and the others always drank in small cups, Ti Frere would fall asleep on the woodbox and come half-awake every time one of them laughed or slapped a winning card down, rattling the cups and the piles of nickels and pennies in front of each man. Then the room would become quieter once more, and his dreams of alligators and owls, ducks and black bears could begin again, always against the dark background of the legendary and unbelievably huge trees.

Finally the game would end, the men would disappear into the night, and Vieux Pop would carry Ti Frere gently to his bed. Octavie would be long asleep by then. She would usually complain about her son's staying up too late, but she always let him have his nights on the woodbox.

Aristile and three of his old buddies—Crapeau Ardoin, Clairmille Trosclair and Placide Laviolette—were playing bourré one cool autumn night, and Ti Frere was sitting in his regular spot, atop the woodbox in the corner, watching and listening. Crapeau Ardoin slapped an ace down and took the winning trick: "Got chou dat time, Steel, you ol' springboard jumper, you!" Aristile glanced quickly at Ti Frere, wondering if he had heard the remark. Ti Frere was looking at Crapeau.

"Yo deal, Steel," Clairmille said. "You better get you mind on de game, ol' buddy, or we gonna take all you catfish money right now." He thumped the worn deck of playing cards lying on the table next to Aristile's small pile of nickels and pennies. "Han' me dat udder deck, Violet," he said to Placide. "Come on! Y'all wanna play bourré, or what?"

"Ti Frere, put dat pot of coffee on de stove and check de wood," Vieux Pop said, a clear note of discomfort in his voice. He glanced at Crapeau and frowned before beginning to shuffle the cards. Crapeau squinted back at him as if to say, "Sorry, Steel, but you gonna have to tell 'im about it one of dese days."

Vieux Pop nodded at Crapeau as though he knew what his old friend was thinking, excusing him for the remark and agreeing with his logic, the wordless nod conveying acceptance of both the unspoken apology and the equally silent advice: He would have to tell Ti Frere someday that he and his old friends had cut down thousands of the big trees. Hundreds of acres of old growth cypress had been leveled by the same four pairs of hands now holding cards at the little square cypress table in Vieux Pop's house on Bayou Goujaune.

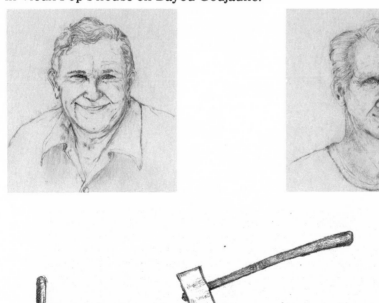

Ti Bird

In spite of his youth, Ti Frere frequently traveled several miles from home in his pirogue, accompanied only by his dog Moccasin and his red-shouldered hawk Ti Bird. He had found the hawk, only a chick then, almost a year earlier. Someone or something, a big wind maybe, had knocked the hawk nest out of a cypress tree, and it had fallen into the water. When Ti Frere came along, he saw a small hawk trying to balance itself on a piece of driftwood to keep from drowning. It was wet and cold and nearly starved.

Ti Frere knew that hawks usually hatched three eggs, but he was unable to locate the other baby birds, so he approached the one he had found, cut small bits of fish and crawfish from his morning's catch and offered one to the bird. At first the little hawk was too frightened or too weak to eat. He only held the piece of fish in his beak and watched Ti Frere and Moccasin, never having been so close to a human or a dog in his short life. Finally he snapped at the piece of fish and swallowed it. Almost immediately the little bird seemed to gain strength and interest in his food. Ti Frere offered him piece after piece, and he gobbled them down quickly until the boy decided he had had enough.

"What will you name it?" Octavie asked when Ti Frere took the hawk into the house. She moved the feathery young thing from the dining table to the window sill so she could set out the supper dishes.

"How about Ti Bird?" suggested Ti Frere, who was trying to learn to use English words. A year earlier he would have said *Ti Zoiseau*.

Ti Bird enjoyed riding around on Ti Frere's shoulder in the few weeks before it learned to fly, and its favorite trick was to make a nest-like arrangement of Ti Frere's thick hair, and sit there surveying the scene. When the boy bent over or moved quickly, Ti Bird would dig its talons into his hair and scalp, to avoid falling off, and Moccasin would bark jealously.

When Big Mom finds out that we have a hawk living in the house, she just about throws a fit. "Baby Girl," she starts in on Mama, "don't you know that's not clean? What are y'all trying to do out there, live like the savages?" That's what she calls Indians.

I go to Big Mom's house after school some days. Sitting in her dining room, I can see the wharf where they tie up the school boat that carries me and the other kids home, those of us who live along the bayous where there's no roads. She always has homemade pie and cold milk, and I can go on eating until they start the engine and begin to untie the boat. Then I jump up and kiss Big Mom on the cheek and run like hell.

"Don't slam the screen door!" she yells, just as I slam the screen door.

Big Mom is always after me about someting. "You remember what I told you, don't you, Alec?" she asks me from time to time. I know what's coming; I pretend total confusion.

"About what, Big Mom?"

"Mais, you were not listening, eh?" she says.

"When? What are you talking about?" I ask.

"If you had been listening, you'd remember. You think you know everything already, you. And you never listen to me...Tu m'ecoutes jamais," she says in French. "Take you some more pie, cher."

"Can I have a glass of milk, Big Mom?" She never tells me what it is I'm supposed to have remembered.

Seeds and Vines

"Ideas are like seeds that grow into vines," Vieux Pop said to Ti Frere one day, as the two fed the milk cow and the chickens. "They are planted by grownups and they push upward like yourself. Some are good; some are harmful and destructive. But it's not always easy to say which are which. They are the ideas that grownups want children to believe. Ideas are like the vines that attach themselves to the trees in the forest. They grow upward as the tree grows. They reach for the light and they compete for light with the tree itself. In the soil where the roots grow, they compete for water and food with the roots of the tree. They can cut out the light and nourishment necessary for the tree's healthy growth. They can eventually destroy the tree. The vine cannot survive without the tree to support it. The idea, also, cannot survive without people to carry it. If it is a good idea and it does not become an obsession, all is well. If it is not a good idea, if it is a prejudice, an intolerance, or a lie, it can destroy the person who carries

it as well as those around him. If there is a tree that you love, here in the yard or out in the woods, you can cut the vines off it, pull them up by their roots even, and let your tree grow well and healthy. But the vines that grow on you are a different matter. It is not so easy sometimes to tear them away, roots and all." While Aristile spoke, Alexson envisioned himself hopelessly tangled in vines, unable to escape or even to move. "As you grow, you will see vines on your friends, and sometimes you will hardly know how to approach them. Not everyone feels the way you do, Ti Frere, about the big woods and the birds and animals. Some of your own friends will disappoint you with their cruelty. Those are some of their vines."

Aristile had traveled to New Orleans once in 1925, and while there he had met a writer named Sherwood Anderson. The Yankee writer and the backwoodsman sat on the big levee bordering the Mississippi River at the French Quarter, and they struck up an easy conversation. The writer spoke of ideas and of his concept of truth, and the swamper spoke of life on the bayou. And so they spent the afternoon talking and watching boats of every size and kind going up and down the wide river before them, while the life of the old city went on as usual behind them. On saying goodbye that evening each man felt that the memory of this experience would never be forgotten.

It was from Sherwood Anderson that Aristile had gotten his concept of seeds and vines and ideas. He always admired the writer, although he could barely read English, and could not, therefore, experience Anderson's stories. Years later, when Octavie and Wilferd went to New Orleans on their brief honeymoon, Octavie had spied a poster in a little shop, and recognized on it the name of Sherwood Anderson as someone Aristile had spoken fondly of having known. She purchased the poster for her father, though Wilferd considered it a waste of his money. In the middle there was a photograph of a wrecked and rusted automobile sitting almost fender deep in a swamp, being absorbed back into the environment, and it was surrounded by cypress trees. Above the photograph were these words: "When Sherwood Anderson said, 'There are many sick trees in the forest,' he was talking about people." Below the photograph: "When Jesus said, 'The meek will inherit the earth,' He was talking about trees."

The poster had hung since that day in Aristile's bedroom, and though he was never so pessimistic as to agree with the second statement, he liked the idea behind the photograph, as well as the analogy between people and trees. There was nothing on the walls of his bedroom but a gunrack and the poster. Before he blew out his old kerosene lamp at night, Aristile would often look up from his bed, and study the poster carefully.

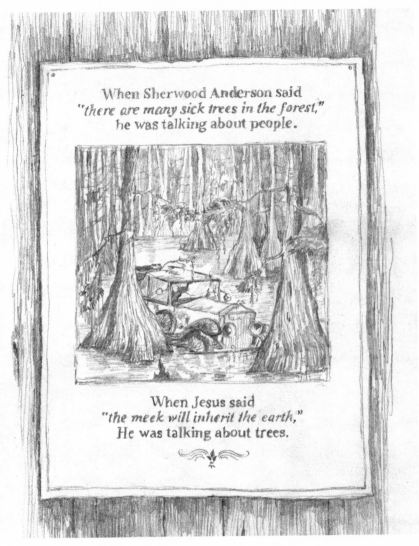

When Sherwood Anderson said *"there are many sick trees in the forest,"* he was talking about people.

When Jesus said *"the meek will inherit the earth,"* He was talking about trees.

Wonder where Sherwood Anderson is now. He was a good man, I think, smart for sure, but restless. Don't think he'd stay en Ville for long...The meek will inherit the earth...What does it mean? Did Jesus say that? Did somebody say that and when somebody else said, Where did you hear that? he said, Jesus said it? Inherit the earth. I-N-H-E-R-I-T. Suffer the meek to come unto me. Come. Come. The time to inherit the earth is upon you. Come and inherit the Atchafalaya.

Trees

Ti Frere often wandered in the Basin during the low water stage of fall. It was a favorite activity for the growing boy. "Why are the stumps so big and the living trees so small?" he asked Vieux Pop, who was cooking a big chicken and sausage gumbo over a low fire at the woodstove.

"In the late 1800s and early 1900s the lumber companies came in and bought the land cheap. To make money on their investment they hired logging crews to cut the trees, for the valuable cypress lumber."

"But, Vieux Pop, why did they cut all the big trees? Why can't I see what the forest looked like? Was it beautiful? Do you remember?"

"Yes, it was beautiful! The trees were magnificent." Vieux Pop began to gesture with his hands; "Most of them were bigger in diameter than the outhouse in our back yard, eighty or ninety feet tall before the first branches, huge columns, straight, round, solid. Standing in a forest of big trees, even at midday, you might have guessed, if you didn't know better, that the light was that of early morning or late afternoon because the huge trunks and leafy branches blocked out so much of it. There was a canopy a hundred feet up that looked like the ceiling of a great cathedral."

"The trees were so close together that it was difficult in some areas to travel through the swamp in anything but a small pirogue." Aristile was transported by memory back to the great forest.

"But why did they cut down all the trees?" Ti Frere insisted.

"Well, it was a business, you know. The companies that had bought the swampland wanted to make money by selling the lumber. Those people didn't live here, and they didn't care about the future," Vieux Pop explained. "Old cypress was a very valuable wood. You could build anything with it—boats, houses, barns, furniture, barges, water tanks, fence posts, anything. It was easy to work and durable." And then he continued, in Cajun English: "Well, you know, Ti Frere, not'ing lasses fuh evah, not even somet'ing big an' strong like dose ol' tree."

Vieux Pop gets a sad look on his face that I can never quite understand. He is looking right through me, as if I'm not even there anymore. What is he seeing? The big trees maybe? Some memory from his youth? I try to bring him back: "I'll be able to see the big trees one day, won't I, Vieux Pop, if I live to be as old as you?"

"No, no! Not hif you live to be twice as old like me. Every lass one of dose big tree was older den 500 year. Some was older den 2,000 year. No, nevah again. Hit's too late." Then he sometimes walks outside to chop firewood, or clean his nets, or repair something; and I know that the talk is ended. Sometimes I know, too, that he is close to tears. I wonder why he gets like that.

"Why didn't you stop them, Vieux Pop? Why didn't you just make them stop?" he repeated. It was Ti Frere's belief that his grandfather could do anything he wanted—could solve any problem, right any wrong.

"There were times when fishing and moss-picking didn't supply enough money for those who lived on the bayou—times when fish would not get into the nets. At other times, there was plenty fish, but the buyers paid so little for them that it was pointless to catch the fish and take them to market, because the fishermen were working hard only to lose money.

I remember days when you couldn't have found twenty-five cents in this house. Plenty days were like that. Then the land company men came to the fishermen and said, 'We own these swamps covered with cypress trees. We will pay you well, if you work for us. Cut these trees, float the logs out to the mills that we're building along the edges of the swamp.'

"So the people of the swamp said, 'All right, we love the trees, but there are so many of them. It won't really make any difference.' Everywhere you looked there were huge old cypress trees, so they told themselves and each other, 'O.K., we will do this thing for a certain time. We'll cut the trees, make some money, buy some better clothes to replace our rags, a new shotgun to provide food for the table. We'll buy nets and crawfish traps and boat engines and fuel so that we might have a better chance to make a living fishing.' But once they had started cutting the trees, there was no end to it. They couldn't seem to find a way to stop. They earned enough to buy not only the things they needed, but even to save some money. They were not wise, Ti Frere. They didn't know or didn't want to know that north of them in the swamp and south of them and in every direction there were logging crews like theirs cutting the trees. So they cut and cut, and they let themselves forget that the great trees were many hundreds of years old and that the beauty and tranquility and peace they provided, as well as safe homes for wildlife, would all be gone—forever.

"Without realizing the meaning of what they were doing, they themselves changed the great cypress forest into cutover swampland. We, of all people, *they*, I mean, should have known better. They had come to live here because of the big trees and the abundant wildlife that the forest supported. Then they allowed, and even helped the landowners, including the state of Louisiana, to nearly destroy their chosen homeland. They were not wise; they did not think ahead. They placed the need for having jobs and making money above the value of the big woods. For the landowners it was a business; for my friends it was a job; for you it is a loss that can never be corrected, *never*.

"The swamp is beautiful now; you know it is, and you know that I've said to you more than once, 'I wish you could have seen the swamp the way it was when I was a boy.' Yes, it is still a thing of great beauty, and I know that you will someday say to your own children and grandchildren those same words: 'I wish you could have seen the swamp the way it was when I was a boy,' for this place continues to change, to fill up with sand and silt that come into the Basin from the Mississippi River. And it has become more and more a victim of people who don't understand, people who litter and who destroy things, people who lessen the quality of a place by their presence alone.

"One standing tree like those I've told you about could provide homes for hundreds of creatures: squirrels, raccoons, wood ducks, hawks, herons, owls, song birds, tree frogs, lizards, woodpeckers. Imagine a tree 180 feet tall, six feet in diameter—what a creation this is! When they cut the trees, they didn't think about the effect it would have on the wild creatures living in them, nor on ourselves who lived below them."

Vieux Pop sends me out for wood, but I know what he's doing. He's getting rid of me so I can't see him crying, but I saw already. I saw one big ol' tear rolling down his face, takin' a crooked path through his beard stubble and fallin' right in the gumbo. I even heard it; that's how quiet it was just before I stepped through the doorway.

If one of my buddies at school had seen that, it'd be all over for me. Shame, shame, Ti Frere's grandfather is a crybaby. So much for his reputation as the toughest man on the bayous, and so much for my reputation as anything.

To Save a Giant

"I heard this story from some of the men who were there, and I believe that it is true," Aristile said to Alexson one fall day, as they chose a comfortable place to sit at the base of the big live oak in the front yard. They had been splitting and stacking firewood, and it was time for a rest and a good opportunity for Vieux Pop to share with Ti Frere one of his favorite memories. "Listen well, Ti Frere. This story may help you in more ways than one someday.

" There was once a stand of cypress trees even bigger than the others, on state land in Buffalo Swamp several miles south of here, and there was a crew cutting the trees for a lumber company. It was this time of year, if I remember correctly, yeah, mid-November, back in 1890. The water was low, the way it always is in the fall, and the crew had been working in that area for five or six weeks. Two good men could drop a tree of six or seven-foot diameter in about half an hour. The place was covered with the big logs, their tops and branches having been cut off by another crew. As soon as the river began to rise in December and flood the swamp, the logs would be floated out, gathered into rafts in the river and pulled to the sawmill.

"At that time logging crews lived in floating camps and didn't come out of the woods for weeks at a time; it was a rough life. One morning when the crew was nearing the end of its work in that area, they came upon a cypress tree that was considerably bigger and taller than all the rest—a giant among giants—and the men looked at it with wonder; none of them had ever seen a tree that size. They delayed cutting the tree, which was near the center of a small clearing in the swamp, purposely leaving it for last.

"Because it was not badly crowded by other trees, it had grown straight and tall, and its massive branches extended far out in all directions. Like many of the biggest trees, this one served as home for all kinds of birds and animals. Squirrels ran and jumped from branch to branch. Raccoons

hid behind moss and leaves, peeking down on the men as they worked the saws and axes, always coming closer. Owls perched on the lower branches, watching quietly. Hawks on the topmost branches looked over a scene totally unfamiliar to them—miles and miles of trees that had always towered to great heights above the swamp floor now lay flat and useless. Egrets and ibis came and went nervously, and songbirds with no other trees to land on filled the branches of this last tree. The air itself around the giant cypress was a swarm of birds and butterflies.

"As the time for cutting the big tree came closer, one of the men, Choupique LaCouture it was, began talking quietly to the others, out of hearing of the company boss, about an idea that had come to him earlier that day. 'You already saw a tree that big, you?' he asked one of the other loggers. "Not me, no,' the man replied. 'Well, OK, then,' Choupique said, as if having reached a conclusion of some kind.

Choupique had been injured the day before when a falling branch struck him on the right shoulder, causing a severe bruise. The boss had reluctantly given him a couple of days off to get well, and 'stop wasting company time,' as he put it. Choupique passed the time counting the annual rings on the stumps of fallen trees, trying to discover which of them had reached the greatest age.

"'Eight hundred and ninety-six,' he yelled from the top of an average-sized stump. Half an hour later he yelled again: "One thousand four hundred and forty-seven!' An hour or so later he announced: 'One thousand six hundred and eighty-four!' Each time he found a new champion, the men would cheer and point to this or that stump, claiming that it could easily beat the current leader. Choupique would lie on his stomach with his head at the stump's center and begin counting. 'One hundred,' he would say, with his finger only a couple of inches from the center. Cypress trees standing so close together grew very slowly, and a hundred years of growth could be measured in only an inch or two of diameter," said Aristile. "'Two hundred,' he would announce a little later and further from the center. None of the other men would pay attention until he got over a thousand. Then they would begin betting a few nickels and dimes among themselves, as to whether a particular tree would beat the 1,684-year-old one, trying to judge, from Choupique's position on the trunk, how many rings might still remain to be counted. Just give Cajuns something to bet on, and they're as happy as a sac-a-lait in a school of minnows. Cajuns that don't like to bet are as rare as feathers on a catfish." Aristile smiled to himself.

"Some of the big trees were so close to one another that an agile man could sometimes jump from the springboard on one tree to the springboard on the next tree. The game was to see how many solid blows of an axe he could put into the second tree before the first one had finished falling and crashing into the shallow water around it, seeming to shake the entire earth. As soon as his partner would yell, 'Timber!' the springboard jumper, who never wore shoes, would grab his axe and leap for the nearest board, having chosen it beforehand. His axe would be flying toward the huge trunk even before he was safely perched on the board, and he would whack it as many times as he could while the first tree tottered and began to fall, its many tons of solid wood speeding faster and faster toward the ground.

"As you can probably guess, Ti Frere, there were some quick bets made on how many axe blows the logger could make before the tree had completed its fall, and constant arguments about whether the tree had finished falling before or after the last axe blow. 'He hadn't even begun his swing,' one man would declare. 'Are you kidding?' another would ask. 'He was already pulling back for the next swing.' The record was seven blows; some said eight.

"Anyway, when all the biggest trees, except the one that stood alone, had been cut, Choupique found a stump nearby that had 1,829 annual rings."

"Vieux Pop," Ti Frere interrupted, "how do you know so many details about something that happened so long ago?" Aristile had gotten so wrapped up in his story, he nearly forgot, from time to time, that he was talking to Ti Frere. "And a little while ago, you said that Mister Choupique had an idea about something while he was counting the tree rings, but you never told me what it was."

Aristile ignored the question about knowing all the details. He shifted his position, watched a great egret spear a minnow in the shallow water across the bayou, and continued his story: "Choupique's idea was that the logging crew should not cut down the biggest tree. It was too beautiful, too big, too unusual. Felling it would be wrong, he thought, and the other men were ready to agree with him, but the lumber boss was not. It was his job to get as many logs to the mill as possible, and to leave the biggest tree out in the swamp was not something he would consider. But Choupique insisted: 'What's one tree?' he asked. 'Who's gonna know

anyway? We already got thousands of logs ready to float to the mill.' The boss was not a man who was used to having his authority challenged, and Choupique was in danger of losing his job when one of the other men yelled, 'Lunch time,' and the problem was put aside for a while.

"The men walked to their pirogues and pulled out salt pork sandwiches that had been prepared for them that morning by the camp cook, and they sat on stumps to eat. Choupique and some of the others settled on the stump of the 1,829-year-old tree, and Choupique began to count again, this time from the outside ring. 'O.K.,' he said, 'here we are—1890.' He made a mark on the outermost ring with the logger's pencil that he always carried, though the outside edge of the tree would have been mark enough. The other men, these cutters of ancient trees, looked on as though they had never before seen annual rings. Choupique counted back twenty-five rings and made a mark: 'End of the Civil War, 1865,' he said. The two marks were less than an inch apart. He counted off sixty-five more rings and made a mark: 'Turn of the century, 1800.' He counted again and put a mark at 1765: '1765—the Acadians invade South Louisiana!' he announced. Some of the men laughed; others clapped and cheered.

" 'Come ahead back,' Choupique told himself as he moved toward the tree's center, marking each century and historic date as he came to it. 1492 got an extra heavy mark. Most of the men had finished eating and some were napping briefly, waiting for the boss to order them back to work.

The others counted silently along with Choupique, and watched as he made his mark for each century backward in time. Finally he said aloud, 'One thousand eight hundred and twenty-nine.' He took a scrap of yellowed paper from his pocket and did a calculation with his marking pencil. Then he put a finger on the exact center of the big tree's heart. 'I, Choupique LaCouture, am touching something today whose life began in the year 71 A.D.,' he said, and he left his finger there for several seconds, as if to gain something from the experience. No one else spoke nor moved. Even the birds in the big tree had gone silent. The stillness woke the two men who had been nodding off to sleep, and they raised themselves on their elbows and looked at Choupique. 'What's happening?' one of them asked. No one answered. Finally the boss spoke, and the spell was broken: 'Work time,' he said.

"Two or three of the men were still staring at the exact center of the big stump, and they found it difficult to move. One man picked up his axe and prepared to get down from the stump, but first he reached over and touched the place where Choupique's finger had been. '71 A.D.' he said. One after another, the men touched the spot, some in wonderment, others not wanting to miss whatever benefit might result. The boss laughed at the men: 'You Cajuns,' he said. 'Superstition starts just under your thick hides, doesn't it?'

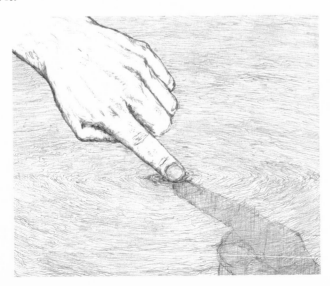

"'Don't have nothing to do with being Cajun,' Choupique said. 'And as far as superstition goes, you don't know everything. Nobody knows everything.' Then he said something in French and turned away.

"The boss let the insult pass, since it had been spoken softly, and he could pretend that he hadn't heard it. Besides, he didn't want to have to admit that he couldn't speak their language to men who had learned to speak his, and he was eager to get the crew to work again.

"It was one of those cool, bright days in the fall, and Wilson knew that he could push the men much harder on a day like this than he could on the oppressively hot days of summer. He was ready to finish with the big tree and move on to destroy another part of the forest. Choupique wouldn't give up, though.

"'We been talkin' it over, Mr. Wilson, and we're gonna leave the big tree like it is,' Choupique said. At first, Wilson thought he had misunderstood. What he thought he had heard made so little sense that it confused him momentarily. But he made a speedy recovery: 'What did you say?' he asked. His disbelief was so thick you could have scraped it off by the pound with a dull axe." Aristile chuckled to himself.

"'I said we're gonna save this tree,' Choupique said, looking into Wilson's eyes without emotion or hesitation.

"'Don't believe I'm hearing well today,' Wilson remarked, sticking an index finger into each ear and shaking it, avoiding Choupique's eyes and smiling broadly at the other men, hoping that this was no more than a joke, and he could go on with the business of lumber production.

"But Choupique was determined: 'Look how much bigger this tree is than the one we were just sitting on. This tree was alive and growing when Jesus Christ was born.'

"'What of it?' Wilson said, 'He wasn't born out here in the damned swamp, was He? He wasn't born in the shade of this tree, was He?'

"'Not talkin' about where He was born,' Choupique said. 'Talkin' about when.'

"'I don't see the connection. This tree didn't know whether Jesus

Christ was born or not and still don't know nothing about it to this day. Cut it down before I lose my temper.'

"'How you know what a tree knows or don't know?' Choupique insisted, as Wilson began walking away.

"'You're fired, Lacucha!' he said, turning on Choupique. 'Pick up your stuff at the camp and move out! Lumber companies don't stay in business by leaving the biggest trees behind, and I don't stay in business by arguing with a bunch of ignorant swampers over whether or not to cut down a tree! The rest of you, get that damned tree down to my level, and I don't mean tomorrow evening!'

"The other men couldn't afford to be fired any more than Choupique could, so two of them walked up to the tree and began preparations to take it down. No one was moving fast, and Choupique hadn't moved at all. The two men at the tree avoided meeting his eyes. One began to sharpen his axe so that he could chop holes to support the springboards. The other began very slowly and deliberately to work on his crosscut saw with a file he always carried in his back pocket. Wilson pretended not to notice the delay. He sat on a nearby stump and began nervously to roll a cigarette. The rest of the crew stood around and watched. One man began to whittle on a wood chip with his pocket knife. Tension was high, and no one had the courage to break it by speaking. The only sound in the swamp was that of two files brushing steel, one on the axe, one on the saw. Finally, Wilson had had enough: 'You gonna chop them springboard holes, or you gonna work that axe bit till it's all filed away?' Choupique looked away from the tree. The man with the axe stepped up quickly to the ancient trunk, chose a location for the first hole and began his swing. The bit was a blur at the end of the powerful man's axe handle, but instead of biting into the sapwood of the big tree, it flew off and imbedded itself three inches deep in the stump where Wilson was sitting, missing his hand by an inch where it rested on the edge of the stump, the cigarette it held still unlit. All eyes were on the sharpened bit and the spared fingers next to it. Axe bits could fly off at any time, but these men were more careful than most, and no bit of theirs had ever left the handle."

"Wilson recovered quickly. To him nothing had meaning beyond itself. Not the strange silence, the men's crazy request, nor the flying bit had shaken him. He jumped down from the stump and said, to no one in particular, 'Give me an axe!'

" ' Take mine,' Choupique offered, smiling as though he knew something that Wilson didn't.

" ' Didn't I tell you to leave?' Wilson asked.

" ' I want to see you cut down this tree first, Mr. Wilson, sir.' The silence was still so complete that the spoken exchange seemed unnaturally loud.

"Wilson grabbed the axe, spun on his boot heel and charged toward the tree. He tripped over a cypress knee and fell, and it was as he was starting to rise that lightning struck nearby and a deafening crack and a roar of thunder shook the ground and electrified the air itself. The men were stunned by the sudden noise and blinding light."

"Almost immediately a drenching rain began to fall, and everyone ran for whatever rain gear was stored in the nearby pirogues. Wilson stumbled again, this time at the base of the huge tree, and dropped the axe. Choupique stepped up and retrieved it, never once looking at Wilson, who by that time was soaked and shivering in the driving windstorm that accompanied the rain. Even the tree, in spite of its immense size, swayed a little in the powerful wind. Wilson realized that the men were leaving, going back to camp to escape the storm, and he knew that making them cut the tree down now would be impossible.

"Once they reassembled at the logging camp, not one man could remember having seen any buildup of clouds or wind before the storm hit, but in the heat and tension of the argument at the base of the giant cypress, the coming storm could have crept in unnoticed, they decided.

"Wilson had begun to fear the big tree, and whatever mysterious powers seemed to protect it, and he never returned to the Buffalo Swamp. When the water rose and the float crew entered the area that winter to collect the logs lying everywhere, they marvelled at the size of the lone cypress tree and at the axe bit stuck into the nearby stump. They gathered the logs into floating rafts, four to six logs wide and a hundred yards long, and began to move them by towboat toward the company sawmill near a little town on the western edge of the swamp.

"The story of the big tree and what happened there that day in 1890 circulated among crews in the logging camps throughout the Basin. No one could say with any certainty whether the occurrences on that day were the result of coincidence or of powers beyond human control, but there were many theories. Some people made the long trip into the depths of the swamp to see the tree and the axe head imbedded in the stump a few feet away. Some even put their hand where they thought Wilson's hand had been, near the steel bit, but no one tried to remove it, and it's probably still there now. Usually they would touch the big tree and then leave, and after a while people stopped going, the logging crews moved to other, distant stands of cypress, and the story was mostly forgotten."

"What happened to Mr. Choupique, Vieux Pop?"

"Well, he quit logging and went back to fishing for a couple of years, and then he moved away."

"Vieux Pop," Ti Frere said, "when you started telling me the story of the big tree, you said it might help me in more ways than one someday. I don't understand."

"I said that for two reasons. One is that I want you to know something that I came to realize only after many years: Nothing is certain; nothing really important is completely understandable and clear. Some things happen for which there is no easy explanation, and sometimes there is no explanation at all. We never are able to see all sides of a thing at once. We think we know and understand something completely, and we act according to that. Days or even years later we find that our thinking was wrong, and our actions based on that thinking were wrong too. Life is always a mystery—always. Do you understand what I'm trying to say?"

"I don't know, Vieux Pop. I'll think about it. What's the other reason you told me the story?"

"You're growing up and I know that every year you go further and further from this house alone in your pirogue, except for Moccasin and Ti Bird. I know too that you get lost from time to time and find your way back without help. But you're still not very far from home and after a while you find yourself in familiar surroundings. The Buffalo Swamp is a different thing, though. It seems endless. Once you get into it, you begin to find that everything looks the same, but nothing is really familiar. After a while you will begin to think you know the place well enough to find your way out; that's when you get really careless, and suddenly you're hopelessly lost. You can lose track of time and direction. On an overcast day you have no idea at all where the sun might be. The sky is the same grey color and brightness everywhere. You could panic and never find your way out.

"If you ever get lost in that area, this is what I want you to do: Find the tallest tree that you can climb, and climb as high as you can. It may be one of the big hollow trees that have stood there since before the logging crews came through—like one of those you feel woodpeckers pounding on."

Ti Frere was surprised: "You've seen me do that? Did you think I was crazy?"

"No! No. I tried it myself after I saw you do it. It's a good feeling, but I never would have done it if I hadn't seen you standing there one day with your head against a hollow tree. I couldn't figure at first what you were doing. Then I heard the woodpecker, and it all began to make sense. You have more love and feeling for the wilderness than anyone I ever knew." Ti Frere smiled.

"Anyhow, find a tall tree you can climb, and look in every direction until you see the big tree. If you can't see it, go a mile or two further, climb another tree and look again. You'll know it for certain when you see it, because it's twice as tall as any tree around, even those that were too small to cut in the late 1800s and have had fifty years to grow since then. When you see it, mark its location clearly in your mind, climb down and begin paddling in that direction. If you don't come to it after a time, climb another tree, find the big one again and go to it. When you get there, you'll see a pathway or clearing going straight away from it. That open waterway goes directly west, and it was made by the float crews hauling thousands of big logs to the wide bayou, called Six Hundred Dollar Bayou, that flows by the sawmill.

"After paddling three or four miles in this opening you will pass through an area of strange-looking live oak trees. The oaks grew on ridges of clam shells left centuries ago by Indians who lived in the Atchafalaya Basin. But flood waters in 1912 and 1927 washed most of the shells away, and now the big oaks are suspended above the ground on their massive roots. You can paddle your pirogue right under the trunks themselves, through the roots that extend for many yards in all directions. When you see these trees, you'll know that you are about halfway out of Buffalo Swamp."

Ti Frere tried to imagine the strange oak trees his grandfather had described, and the great mysterious cypress tree: "Could you show me some day soon?" Ti Frere asked.

"Yes, I surely could, maybe next spring when the water rises and it's easy to travel by boat through the swamp. I always intended to show it to you anyway."

All I would have to say is, "The axe bit that nearly cut off Wilson's fingers was mine." I must be crazy to keep telling the boy about the old days and the big trees. The more I teach him to love my memory of what it was like, the more he will hate me for what I did. I can recognize the ghost of an old lie as well as any man, but I can't bring myself to tell him that I was a logger. I cannot be what I am not, until I am. I almost wish Wilferd had told him before he disappeared. He was mean enough to do it. He could have hurt me in the boy's eyes by telling him, but he had so little respect for the trees himself, it probably never crossed his mind that anyone else could care about their loss, even Ti Frere. The man never knew his own son.

A Photograph

One damp Saturday morning later that month, while Aristile was running hoopnets on the river and Octavie was outside washing clothes on her scrubboard, Ti Frere, who had been confined to the house because of a lingering cold, began rummaging through an old chest in his mother's room.

There was a yellowed wedding dress that had once been snow-white; there were two old albums of black and white photographs, some of his mother and father's wedding, a few of himself as a baby and as a young boy. There were boxes of letters and buttons and some very cheap jewelry that Wilferd had given to Octavie fourteen or fifteen years earlier. And there was an old cardboard box way at the bottom under some blankets and some of Wilferd's clothing that Octavie had kept, thinking he might return some day.

Ti Frere loved old pictures. It was his way of knowing what things were like in the years before he was born; and to his delight, he found the little box to be full of very old photographs. He sat comfortably on the floor next to the big chest and began to look closely at the pictures, putting a few aside because he wanted to ask his mother or grandfather something about them. Then he came to one that stopped him. It was upside-down, and he turned it in his hand slowly, for a chill was creeping through his spine, almost as though he knew what he had discovered even before he saw it clearly.

A group of young men is sitting on top of a big cypress tree stump with their crosscut saws, wedges and axes. A huge tree they felled lies in the shallow water behind them, its branches still covered by Spanish moss. One of the men is unmistakeably Vieux Pop, and there is no question in my mind what he is doing there. He's holding an axe in one hand and one end of a crosscut saw in the other. He's smiling as I've seen him smile thousands of times, when he's done or seen something that satisfies him. Besides that, his name, Aristile, is written on the edge of the photograph, and the date October 1903. Two other names are written there—Placide and Crapeau—two of Vieux Pop's card-playing buddies. How could it possibly be? I hope it's some kind of mistake, but I know it's not.

How many times has he told me about the beauty of the big woods, the trees that grew so thick that they nearly shut out the light of the midday sun, the massive trunks so close together that in some areas it was difficult for a man to travel among them in anything larger than a small pirogue? He goes on and on about how he wishes that I could have somehow seen the swamps as they were in the late 1800s and early 1900s. His descriptions are so fine that I can see the great forest taking shape before my eyes, and my heart beats with excitement. But he was a logger himself, a swamper. Vieux Pop is one of the men who cut down all the big trees.

Ti Frere put the photograph aside and then replaced all the other things back into the old trunk, just where he had found them. When he had finished, he closed the lid and left the room. Then he sat on the front porch, with the photograph in his hand, and waited for his grandfather to return.

When Aristile came back down the bayou later that morning, he didn't see Alexson until he had pulled his boat alongside the small wharf and tied it. By the time he looked up, the boy was walking toward him.

"Hey, Ti Frere; how you feeling today, my boy?" Alexson didn't answer. He walked slowly up to the wharf and looked into the boat. The fish were separated into two holds—catfish in one, gaspergou and buffalo in another. And there was a five-gallon can full of brightly-colored blue crabs. Aristile wondered why there had been no response. "Hey, look at this," he said. "Got me about a sixty-pound yellow cat in that deep hole near Bird Island. You want to help me get him into the livebox?"

Still Alexson said nothing. He looked at Aristile, then at the photograph he had held in his hand all morning. Aristile waited, confused. Suddenly Alexson crumpled the old photograph with both hands and threw it at his grandfather, hitting him hard in the face. Then he turned and ran into the house.

Aristile retrieved the photograph from where it had landed on the floor of his boat, and as he did, he heard the door of Alexson's room slam shut. Slowly he lowered himself to sit on the edge of the boat, and he smoothed the photograph against his leg. He looked at it for a long time, studying and remembering every detail, all the while wondering how he would go about trying to explain to Alexson what he and his friends had done. He put the photograph carefully into the pocket of his raincoat and began unloading his catch, first the scale fish, into a section of the livebox on the opposite side of the narrow wharf. When he dropped the sixty-pound catfish into the livebox, he looked up and saw that Octavie was sitting on the edge of the porch, watching him.

"Nice bunch of fish, Pop," she said. "But I'm afraid you've got some serious explaining to do to your grandson."

Over and over again years later I would recall how sad it had been the day I lost faith in Vieux Pop. There was no way in the world then that I could have understood what he had done. In my eyes Aristile Guilbeau might as well have dropped every tree himself, single-handedly, dancing barefoot from springboard to springboard, diabolically wielding some sort of magical evil axes and saws.

Alienation

Two days after finding the photograph of Aristile and his logging buddies, Ti Frere couldn't stand to be in that house with his mother and grandfather any longer.

From its place on the wall over his bed, he took his single-shot 20-gauge Remington, the one Vieux Pop had taught him so carefully to use to provide food for the family. He opened a drawer of the little chest that held most of his possessions, a chest made of old red cypress. It had been constructed for him by Aristile when he was only a few days old, the beautiful piece of furniture intended to honor the baby's having come into the world. There was a half-empty box of shotgun shells in the drawer, and Ti Frere put three of them into his pants pocket. He purposely left the drawer open and walked through the room where his mother sat knotting a hoopnet in one corner while his grandfather polished his favorite old leather hunting boots. No one spoke, but Aristile's eyes followed Ti Frere down the worn back steps and to the beginning of one of the hunting trails that began just beyond the fence surrounding their yard.

"He's going hunting, you think?" Octavie asked, watching Aristile's eyes. She had not stopped working on the net.

"Don't think so," he said. "We'll see."

In less than two minutes, they heard a shotgun blast only a hundred yards into the woods. Aristile and Octavie glanced at each other, then went back to their work.

Ti Frere walked over to the big swamp rabbit he had shot, picked it up by its back legs and felt the last quiver of life leave its soft body. Then he threw the dead creature into a pool of water at the base of an old cypress stump and walked away. He would look for more serious game now, a barred owl, a great blue heron, or one of those big pileated woodpeckers he had admired for years. He was not hunting well now, for his step was neither slow nor quiet, and tears had begun to form in the corners of his eyes. He brushed them away roughly and went on, toward one of the dead trees that he knew the woodpeckers liked to work on. Ti Frere could hear two of them pounding on the big trunk long before he got to a place where he could see them clearly about sixty feet above his head.

Instead of creeping up to the old tree and leaning his forehead against it the way he had always done before, he swung the gun up and took aim at one of the unsuspecting birds. He cocked his gun slowly, never losing aim, and squinted down the long barrel. "Take the time to aim carefully," he could hear his grandfather say, "Squeeze the trigger firmly..." Ti Frere heard the voice so clearly that he thought Vieux Pop might be standing right behind him; he spun around, to find no one. Carefully he took aim again and began to squeeze the trigger slowly and firmly. Then tears burst from his eyes and he lowered the gun quickly, angrily, and uncocked it. He sat at the base of the big tree, wiped his eyes dry, and removed the shell from the barrel of his gun. The woodpecker had gone quiet, and Ti Frere gazed around himself in a daze, not clearly aware of what he was doing or thinking. His eyes were glassy, and it seemed as though everything he saw, the leaves and branches, Spanish moss and tree trunks, was at an equal distance from him, the way faraway objects seemed to be brought into one flattened plane by the lenses of powerful binoculars.

The boy neither moved nor blinked his eyes, and it was only when the woodpecker began pounding again on the tree and Ti Frere could feel the vibrations in his back that the scene was destroyed and his view of the physical world returned to normal.

Ti Frere walked home slowly, unsure of what he would do next. He entered the house quietly and found it empty. Octavie was outside hanging clothes on the line that ran from the chicken coop to a young oak tree, and Vieux Pop was off somewhere in his putt-putt. It surprised Ti Frere to realize that he had not heard the loud old engine start up, for he had surely been close enough to hear it cough to life.

He stepped into his room and dropped the two unused shells into their box and slid the drawer closed. Then he replaced the shotgun on its rack and lay face down on his bed. Just before falling asleep, exhausted by the emotional strain and confusion, Ti Frere felt again the small movement of the dying rabbit in his hands. He raised his head and looked around as if he sensed a familiar presence in his room; then he sank his head into the feather-filled pillow and slept.

When he awoke toward late afternoon, it was to the pleas of the cow that needed milking. He left the house without speaking to Aristile or Octavie, who were both inside by then, and he milked the cow and fed her and her calf without thinking about what he was doing. When Ti Frere returned to the house, there was a plate of hot food waiting for him on the table. Without slowing his step, he put the bucket of milk on the table, picked up his plate and took it outside.

I eat my meals on the front porch now, ever since I learned the truth.

I want to make sure that he knows I'm avoiding him. Let him suffer for cutting the trees and for lying to me. What do I care? I can see, in the corner of my eye, that he and my mother are looking at me. They're worried. Well, let them worry.

Before sunrise the next morning, Ti Frere made an impulsive decision. Without anything other than the clothes he wore, the boy stepped into his pirogue, called Moccasin to join him and began paddling down the bayou. Ti Bird was sitting in his favorite spot at the front of the boat, ready to fly off and inspect anything that interested him. Aristile had left earlier that morning to raise hoopnets he had set in river the previous afternoon.

Ti Frere had no particular destination in mind; he needed only to get away. He paddled on and on for miles, unaware of time or place, and when the little bayou ran into a swamp, he followed it, though he didn't know whether he had ever seen that swamp before. He didn't think about that, for he was lost in disturbing thoughts, and his own safety was of no concern to him.

Aristile returned later that morning with his catch of gaspergou, buffalo and catfish, and as soon as he had rounded the bend in the bayou that allowed him to see his house, he knew that something was wrong. Octavie was sitting on the front porch, staring at the water, rocking slowly in an old chair that Aristile had made for his wife half a century earlier. It was the same chair Octavie had used to try to rock away her sorrow after Valsin drowned, the one she sat in day after day waiting for Wilferd to return from his last poaching trip. Aristile didn't say anything to her until he had transferred the fish to the liveboxes next to his wharf in the bayou.

"It may be bad luck to sit in that chair," he suggested.

"You knew he would run away, didn't you?" she said. She kept on rocking, never looking at him, her eyes fixed on the water. There was a light drizzle, and the surface of the bayou was a constant movement of small, concentric circles of overlapping ripples, appearing and vanishing almost instantly under the circles of new raindrops. Octavie seemed hypnotized.

"Yes, I knew. You knew too. We could not have stopped him if we'd tied him up and locked him in the cowshed. It's something he needed to do." It was over an hour before the light rain stopped and Octavie emerged from her trance. She set up her wash tub on the front porch, instead of in its usual place behind the house, and she began methodically to rub one piece of clothing after another on the scrubboard, alternately watching her father and the bayou that ran slow and deep before her.

Aristile occupied himself with various time-consuming jobs. He split firewood, mended torn nets, patched a small hole in his pirogue, and filled the fuel tank in his putt-putt fishing boat, knowing that he would be taking a trip soon. But he was worried and distracted by his knowledge that

Ti Frere had rejected him and was probably lost by now. He had planned to play cards and fry catfish at Crapeau Ardoin's house two miles up the bayou that evening, but when Crapeau came by for a cup of mid-afternoon coffee on his way to setting his hoopnets, Aristile told him of Ti Frere's leaving, and cancelled the card game and fish fry.

"You were right, Mr. Crop," Aristile said. "I should have told him myself one quiet evening when I had time to explain how things were in those days. But I waited, and he found an old picture of you and me and the rest of the gang at the logging site, and it surprised him so much, he wasn't able to handle it. He met me at the bayou bank with that damned picture when I came in from raising my nets. He crumpled it up and threw it at my face.

"Then he ran and closed himself up in his room. Not telling him was a bad mistake. I guess I figured that when he was a little older, he might be able to understand better." He paused: "No, it's not that. It's just an excuse I tell myself for what I know I should have done." The two old friends finished their coffee in silence, sitting on the edge of the front porch, their feet resting on the ground.

"The boy loves you, Steel. He would have understood well enough, I think. As well as we can understand it ourselves, anyway. You could explain it all to me sometime, too, if you think you can." Crapeau walked to his boat, got in and shoved off.

"You're a good man, Steel," he yelled back. "And you're lucky I won't be taking your money at the bourré table tonight, my friend. Keep your accordion warmed up and we'll play some music next time." Aristile watched until Crapeau Ardoin's boat had entered the first bend in the bayou before returning to his work.

Perdue

Alexson paddled on, hardly noticing any of the details of his surroundings. Egrets and herons watched him as they caught minnows in the shallow water. Nutria and mink swam aside to make room for the big pirogue containing a boy, a dog and a hawk. A black panther crouched on a low cypress branch, hoping that the strange crew might come his way. Ti Frere didn't see the big animal, though he passed only twenty yards from where the panther waited quietly. Moccasin smelled the wildness and began to growl in warning. Ti Bird flew off to have a look at the panther from above, but Ti Frere remained unaware of the creature's presence and of the danger that had been avoided simply by chance, until he had passed it by and the panther let out a scream of frustration. Ti Frere jumped, turned around, and stopped to look at an animal he had heard of but had never seen, a wild creature from his dreams of the old days.

The realization that he was lost crept up on the boy slowly, as a panther would creep up on a fawn. He knew it was lurking there before he allowed himself to think about it, and even then he pushed the thought aside as if it were of no interest to him. But as the day wore on, light began to fade, and his tired muscles began to ache, he finally let himself stop and look around. The thought of being hopelessly lost began to sink in, and Ti Frere felt an emptiness in the pit of his stomach that he knew was fear.

The momentum of his paddling had carried his pirogue into a small opening among the trees. Ti Frere lay back on the bottom of the boat, exhausted, and stared up at the heavily clouded sky. Moccasin licked the bottoms of the boy's feet and whined, unsure of how to approach Ti Frere, who was acting unlike himself. There was a fine mist in the air, almost a drizzle.

This is just the kind of day Vieux Pop described as being easy to get lost on—there's no more light in one direction than in any other. I'd be lost even if the sun were shining brightly. I have no idea how long I've been traveling or in which direction. As my dad used to say, "Pirogues don't leave no tracks." I may have been going in circles for the last hour or more. This must be Buffalo Swamp.

Moccasin is licking my feet: It's beginning to tickle, but I'm too tired to pull them away. I can only move them from side to side to show my annoyance. Finally he stops, distracted by a fish or something that has jumped, with a loud splash, near the boat. I can't see Ti Bird from where I'm lying; he must be in a tree or flying around inspecting the unfamiliar territory. "Find me a tall tree to climb, Ti Bird," I yell, and my voice sounds hoarse and strange in the midst of all this silence. Moccasin jumps at the loud sound and retreats to the far end of the pirogue. I'm going to have to do what Vieux Pop told me, climb the highest tree around and begin looking for the giant cypress that Mr. Choupique refused to cut. It would be easy to fall asleep here and rest, but I might not wake up until after dark, and then I wouldn't be able to find the big tree. Moccasin wouldn't let me sleep even if I wanted to.

Ti Frere raised himself on an elbow and looked around, seeing things clearly for the first time since he had left that morning. It was as Vieux Pop had warned: everything looked the same in every direction, young cypress trees here and there, stumps and more stumps, most of them showing the holes that had once held springboards for the swampers to stand on while cutting the helpless giant trees. "How could he do it?" the boy wondered. "How could he tell me about the big trees and how beautiful they were, when he was one of the loggers himself? I don't understand who he is anymore. He lied to me. I hate him. I hate Mr. Crapeau and Mr. Seed and all the others." Ti Frere brushed a big tear roughly from his face, sat up angrily and began to look for a tall dead tree to climb.

The only big trees left were hollow ones and dead ones that contained no boardfeet of lumber and were therefore of no interest to the land company. They were hollow even when the logging crews came through back in the late 1800s, but still they stood there almost unchanged generation after generation, some of them still supporting a few green leaves and live branches. Before long he found a tree that seemed solid enough and tall enough to provide him the view he needed. Ti Bird was sitting on the topmost branch, calling as though he had found the tree and was trying to lead Ti Frere to it. He was only having a good time exploring new territory and had not the slightest idea that they were lost. "If I had Ti Bird's eyes and wings, I wouldn't have to climb any tree," Ti Frere thought wearily. He tied his pirogue to a low branch of the big dead tree and began climbing, patting Moccasin on the head before pulling himself up and out of the pirogue.

The tree was an easy one to climb at first, for there were still many solid branches for Ti Frere's hands and feet, but as he got higher, he sought holes made by woodpeckers and later used by wood ducks for nesting. Once, about forty feet up, he slipped and nearly fell when a branch he was pulling himself up on cracked and he had to grab quickly for a woodpecker hole just under it. Moccasin whined nervously and turned his head slowly from side to side, watching as Ti Frere rested before beginning to climb again. Every few feet he would stop to look around in hope of spotting the big tree, but each time he knew that he would have to climb higher.

Ti Bird watched from above and Moccasin from below as Ti Frere struggled to make his way up the big tree trunk, hoping as he put his hand or foot into a hole that it was empty and not the doorway into the house of an angry raccoon or a poisonous snake. Once he felt something cold when he stretched and put his right hand high above him into a hole, and the shock of it nearly caused him to fall. When he got level with the hole he could see into it and see part of the coils of the creature he had felt. It was a harmless eggsnake, and he watched it for a few seconds in relief, for there was no way to avoid climbing right over the hole if he were to go higher. He knew that these snakes ate many wood duck eggs, but he did not concern himself with that. He saw it as only one of many aspects of nature over which people have no control.

Finally, at about 110 feet, Ti Frere realized that he was above the surrounding treetops. He had climbed higher than necessary, to the very top of the old tree, concentrating so thoroughly on climbing safely that he had forgotten for a while to look around. He began to scan the horizon to his right and to turn slowly until he was looking over his left shoulder, and there, rising fifty or sixty feet above the treetops surrounding it was the upper part of Vieux Pop's giant tree. "What a monster!" he thought. "It must be two miles away, but even from here it's a huge thing." He looked down. "I see it, Moccasin, I see the big one clear as day! It's only a mile or two in that direction." Ti Frere pointed, and the big dog began to bark, excited as the boy was by whatever had caused him to call down. The cloud cover had begun to thin, and Ti Frere could detect a glow in the sky above and behind the big tree that he knew was the light of the setting sun.

To climb down a tree is often more dangerous than to climb up, but having located the giant tree of Aristile's story had given the boy new energy. He was still lost but not without hope, and he descended without incident.

As Ti Frere stepped back into his pirogue, he was met by an excited Moccasin who licked his perspiring face and raced from end to end in the little boat, nearly turning it over. Finally he lay facing the exhausted boy and only wagged his tail. Ti Frere picked up his paddle and realized that there was a tightness that had not yet left his muscles, a tension left over from the danger of his climb down the old tree trunk. He sat and waited until the tightness eased. Then he began paddling slowly in the direction of the fading light, feeling the coolness of the coming night on his still-damp skin.

There were huge stumps everywhere. It was as Vieux Pop had said. The Buffalo Swamp had contained some of the biggest cypress trees in the entire Atchafalaya Basin.

I wonder which ones Vieux Pop cut. And Mr. Clairmille and Mr. Choupique. I wonder where the birds went that used to live in these trees, and the squirrels and raccoons. The geese migrating down from Canada must have thought they were lost; things must have looked as different from up in the sky as they did from down here.

A small flock of wood ducks circled above Ti Frere, and he could hear the whistle of their wings beating the air. They slid into the water at a safe distance from the lonely boy and his dog, and looked back at him as they swam deeper into the woods. The only other sound was that of a pair of distant owls calling to each other and the occasional thump of Ti Frere's paddle on the side of his boat. Then a woodpecker began drumming on a hollow tree to the left. The sound was surprisingly loud because of the deep silence all around it.

Ti Frere paddled on slowly, for he was very tired. He wanted to reach the big tree before complete darkness overtook him, but he knew that the sun had already set. Looking around, though, it seemed to him that the swamp was getting brighter, and when he finally turned to look back in the direction of the tree he had climbed, he found that the sky had cleared

and the swamp was bathed in the yellow light of the biggest full moon he could remember ever having seen. He paddled on with confidence, as the sun's fading glow slowly gave way to the magical blue light of the brightening moon.

When he finally reached a point from which he could see the tree he sought, Ti Frere found it to be even bigger than he had imagined. He put his paddle down and drifted for a moment, struck motionless by a sight that had existed previously only in his dreams and his imagination. The tree seemed to glow in the blue light. "It's unreal. Maybe the moonlight is playing tricks with my eyes," he thought. Ti Frere approched the tree, its base out of the water on a tiny low island. Then he paddled all the way around it, as if to assure himself that it was three dimensional and real. "No wonder Mr. Choupique protected this tree! It would be a sin to destroy a thing like this." Ti Frere noticed that there were no vines hanging from the tree.

He landed his pirogue among the cypress knees at the base of the giant tree and stepped out. He would spend the night here and in the morning try to find the passageway out to Six Hundred Dollar Bayou, the one that Vieux Pop had described.

He stepped up to the massive trunk and ran his fingers over the bark. He rapped on it with his knuckles as though it were a door. He walked all the way around, seeing as many details as the moonlight would allow. Moccasin followed his every step.

Ti Frere returned to his starting point, sat on the ground against the tree, and looked out across the moonlit swamp. Spanish moss waved gently in a light breeze and the water surface shimmered silver all about him. It was only then, in that moment of calm and rest and safety that Ti Frere remembered that he had not eaten since early morning. It was not like him to go off on a long trip without food of some kind. He would stuff it up into the bow of his pirogue under a raincoat where Moccasin and Ti Bird couldn't get at it—a paper bag of cold biscuits or a sweet potato, at least, if not a venison sandwich on his mother's homemade bread, or some fried chicken or something. "How could I be so dumb? Of course, I didn't plan to get lost, but I should have brought some food anyway." It was his stomach talking, he knew, because he remembered easily enough how angry and upset he had been that morning, and food was not on his mind when he paddled away from home. It was on his mind now, though; and he drew his knees up against his chest, hoping to sqeeze his stomach until its emptiness stopped hurting him.

The breeze dropped off, and a fog formed so thick that it condensed on the leaves of the tree and fell like slow-motion raindrops into the water around the little island, plopping loudly in the stillness of the night. An airplane flew high overhead, and Ti Frere followed its sound, though he couldn't see any lights because of the fog.

Maybe it's not running any lights anyway. Maybe it's a German bomber looking for a town to drop its bombs on. It's only three or four years ago, during the war, that we had to turn the lamps down some nights and all the little towns had "blackouts," because they thought that the German planes might be coming over to drop some bombs. It was scary, and I remember being glad that our roof was made of cypress shingles that don't reflect the moonlight the way tin roofs do. We knew a man during that time who had appeared out of nowhere and settled down with his family a mile or so up the bayou from our place. They lived inside an old trading boat pulled up on the bank. He'd come over and borrow tools from us now and then, and we all liked him. He spoke the good French, but we could understand each other pretty well. He turned out to be a spy for the Germans, and he was arrested just before the war ended. A fisherman had seen him hanging around a hollow cypress tree one day, and after he left, the fisherman found all kinds of radio equipment hidden inside the tree. We kept hearing rumors in those days that German submarines were coming up the Atchafalaya River from the Gulf of Mexico and buying fuel from French-speaking people in Morgan City, down near the mouth of the river. I can't believe that.

If a man is a German spy, does that make his wife a spy, too? They had three or four kids. Were they spies? She had twins during the time we knew them. Were the twins spies? Twin spies. Baby spies. Spy babies?

The earth spun on its axis and sped through space, creating and consuming time as it went. Alexson's thoughts turned quickly from the outrageous absurdity of war to the peaceful beauty of nature when he heard, at a great height, the voices of a flock of Canada geese, migrating south to the Louisiana marshes. He could not see them in spite of the night's brightness once the early-evening fog had lifted, but he could hear their pure voices distinctly in the deep silence of the swamp, and he smiled gratefully, for he knew that they were beautiful.

The boy could not sleep. He continued to stare out into the swamp, studying the strange details of the moonlit trees and stumps. He remembered, almost suddenly, that it was in this same Buffalo Swamp that his father had supposedly disappeared. He felt the chill of fear at the thought, and realized that Wilferd had not entered his mind for several days. Earlier that fall he had questioned his grandfather about Wilferd, and now he recalled the conversation:

"Vieux Pop, why does Big Mom call my dad 'that no-good Shell-grave bastard?'" Ti Frere asked Aristile as they walked through the woods one afternoon looking for signs of deer.

"Aw, you know how Big Mom is, don't you? It would be hard to find any man half good enough to please Eulalie Guilbeau."

"But I heard her tell Mama once that if my pop ever crawled out of the swamp alive, she'd finish him off herself." Aristile stopped and pointed to the tracks of an unusually large buck mixed in with the smaller, heart-shaped prints left by several does.

"The buck was walking way behind the females, letting them take all the chances," he said.

"Was my pop a bad man?" the boy asked, refusing to look at the tracks.

"Come and sit with me on this log for a while," Aristile said, pointing to the trunk of a red maple that had been knocked over by a hurricane the preceding September. When the two friends had settled there Vieux Pop began: "It's hard to judge whether a man is good or bad. Your father was the last of eleven children, and the family was poor, poor. Life was not easy, and he had to fight for everything he got, from food on the table to a place to sit in the boat when the family went to town. He got to be a scrapper; he had to be. I knew him when he was growing up. He was always getting into a fight with somebody, the neighbors' kids, his own brothers and sisters. He grew up like that, never getting enough of anything. His dad, your other grandfather, spent lots of days working away from home, wherever he could make a few dollars. Times were very hard.

"Your dad always had big dreams of an easier life. He began doing things that he should not have done. Even when he was just a boy, he would take things from people who had more than his family had. And when he was able to kill more deer than the Shellgraves could eat, he'd shoot an extra one and find somebody who would buy the meat from him. After a while he was taking orders for deer meat, ducks, squirrels, game fish, whatever people wanted to pay for. I might as well tell you that, because somebody else will if I don't, you know?

"Wilferd had spent a good deal of time off in the woods by himself, and he knew where to hunt for animals and birds he could kill and then sell. Wildlife was fairly plentiful and he figured it wouldn't hurt anything if he took more than his share. He was good at it, but the law was always after him, and he got to be a little mean and impatient. He never found the easy life he was always hunting for, you know?

"Will he ever come back, Vieux Pop? Is he dead?" Ti Frere was looking back down the trail on which they had been walking.

"I don't know, boy. I don't think he'll be coming back. But I just don't know."

"Mama never wants to talk to me about him." It was a question.

Aristile said nothing. He looked back down the trail where Ti Frere still had his eyes fixed. There was nothing more he wanted to say about Wilferd Shellgrave.

Dreams

Finally the boy fell asleep with Moccasin snuggled against his back, and with the eyes of scores of quiet birds and animals looking down on them from the branches of their big tree. Ti Bird was sitting on the stern of the pirogue, watching movements of fish in the clear, shallow, moonlit water.

For two or three hours Ti Frere slept soundly, too exhausted to feel any discomfort in the rough place where he lay. Then he was awakened

by the loud, frightened squawk of a great blue heron that had come to perch on its favorite low branch and realized at the last moment that just below it were a boy, a dog, and a pirogue with a hawk. Ti Frere sat up and rubbed his eyes, wondering what it was that had awakened him. Then he turned over and fell asleep again, but this time his sleep was disturbed by dreams. He saw himself standing at the base of the big tree, as he had stood earlier that evening, knocking on the huge trunk as on a door. But this time a doorknob appeared, and the outline of a door. He turned the knob and pulled; the door opened and he stepped into the tree, into a well-lighted room inside the trunk, a room filled with food—cans of Spam and potted meat, packets of unsalted crackers next to tins of the best sardines, platters of boudin sausage and roast duck, rice dressing and buttered sweet potatoes, fried catfish and chicken gumbo, steaming piles of boiled crawfish and shrimp, hot French bread and home-churned butter. Ti Frere ate as he walked from one table to another, never filling up, tasting everything.

There was another room, like a room in his house, and his mother sat there near a window, her heavy work shoes on her feet, a beautiful smile on her face. He stepped up and took her hand, but she seemed not to notice. She was looking across the room to where his father was rummaging through the old chest, searching frantically for something, throwing clothes and papers and old photographs in all directions. Ti Frere looked back at Octavie and realized that she had hidden something from Wilferd and her smile was a clear sign that she knew he'd never find it.

The picture of Vieux Pop and his logging buddies landed at Ti Frere's feet. He picked it up and put it back into the old chest, but his father threw it out again as he searched for the thing he couldn't find. Ti Frere stepped to the window at the back of the room and looked out, but instead of the familiar back yard with clothes line, chicken coop and all, there was an endless body of water with old fashioned sailing boats and seabirds.

When the boy turned around, Wilferd and Octavie were gone, and when he stepped into the first room, all the food was gone. It was like the inside of a hollow tree, but as big as a room in an old English castle he had seen in a magazine photograph at Big Mom's house. He looked for food everywhere, but not one can of potted meat remained, and his stomach hurt him until he woke up and remembered where he was. The bright moon was almost directly overhead. Ti Frere walked to the water's edge and got down on hands and knees, his hands in the water. He lowered his head until his lips broke the surface, and he drank from the shattered reflection of the moon.

Soon he was asleep again. In his next dream Ti Frere was walking on a footpath that crossed a big pasture near the school he attended in the little town. Suddenly there were two road graders flying around, huge motorized graders like the ones he was used to seeing grade the holes out of the gravel and shell road that went by the school. They were flying like crop dusters, but they no more had wings than the regular road graders that he was used to. Then they began dropping pieces of paper that Ti Frere knew contained a message for him, but the wind was blowing them into the trees along the edge of the pasture. When he ran into the woods and tried to find one of the pages, they were gone. Every time he saw one fall through the trees, he tried to catch it, but as soon as it touched the ground, it would disappear. He could never grab one in time. Frustrated and exhausted, his bare feet cut and bruised, he began to cry. Ti Frere awoke sobbing, with real tears running down his face. He knew not what to make of the dream nor why it made him so sad to have missed reading the message.

The lonely boy stood up and walked around the big tree again. He was not only hungry now; he was cold. It was late November, and winter was only days away. He had no extra clothes stored in his boat, but there was an old life jacket that he used as a seat, so he got it out of the pirogue and covered himself the best he could with it as he curled up against the big tree again. Moccasin watched sleepily for a minute; then both of them fell asleep as before.

That night, while Ti Frere struggled with his cold and hunger and his dreams under the giant tree, Vieux Pop paced the rooms of the cabin.

"Can't you settle down, Pop?" Octavie asked. She sat in one corner of the main room making crawfish traps from chicken wire and steel clamps.

"I'm worried," Vieux Pop admitted. "There's nothing we can do now." He began slicing onions at the dining table.

"You said it was OK," she reminded him. "He knows the swamps pretty well, you said. He'll be all right."

"That's what I said, but I'm worried. He's only twelve, and even Wilferd disappeared out there, well as he knew how to handle himself."

"You trying to scare me, Pop?" Octavie asked, concern showing on her pretty face.

"No. I quit," Aristile said. He left the onions and began preparing the woodstove for cooking a venison roast. Sandwiches of venison were among Ti Frere's favorite foods. Roast duck was his favorite of all, but it was still early in the year for duck hunting, and the skillful old cook didn't have any ducks to roast. He knew that he would not be able to sleep that night, and he had begun to find things to do to occupy himself. At first light he would leave for the place on Six Hundred Dollar Bayou where he hoped to find his grandson.

It was after midnight when Octavie, exhausted by work and worry, stopped making traps and prepared for bed. She put her tools and clamps into an old straw basket on the floor beside her chair.

"Take care tomorrow, Pop. I'll be waiting. And I'll be wanting to feed two men here tomorrow evening."

Men? I've already fed two men. Fed myself to them—Valsin and Wilferd. For what? The swamp and the river took both of them. I fed myself to them, and they fed themselves to the river. Now Ti Frere is gone. What can I do? Please, Big God, this is Octavie down here on the bayou. Let my son come home safe, OK?

"Pop, is there anything I can do? I don't know where you're going, and I know you want to go by yourself, but maybe I could go and look for him in another direction."

Aristile looked up from where he was squatting before the cookstove, feeding dry wood into it. He smiled and winked, trying to hide his own apprehension.

"No, Baby Girl, you'd better stay here in case he finds his way back. Otherwise, I think I know where he might be coming out."

Ti Frere's last dream was the strangest. He would ask himself later whether it had been a dream at all. The sky became cloudy and dark, and a strong wind began to blow, with a strange lifelike moan rising and falling at the treetops and along the water's surface. Ti Frere saw himself lying on the ground at the base of the tree, and he saw himself standing with the tree behind him as well. He felt that something was coming his way, something strange and powerful and not as friendly as he would have liked. For what seemed like hours there were only the wind and the moaning sound, sometimes like a whistle, sometimes a groan. Finally an enormous hawk-like bird came gliding slowly through the trees, turning this way and that to miss the trunks and branches, glowing brightly as though lit from the inside.

Ti Frere looked down and there was a bottomless pool at his feet. From the depths there rose a great white fish, each scale glowing like the feathers of the hawk that now circled slowly around the big tree, never taking its eyes from Ti Frere's face. On his right he felt another presence, and he turned to see a deer, a pure white buck standing like a statue at the far edge of the little island. The buck too glowed with an inner light.

None of these creatures was like any that Ti Frere had ever seen, and he began to tremble in fear and to push back against the big tree. He felt that the hawk was going to swoop down at him, but there was no place to hide. The big fish was rising toward the surface of the pool at his feet, and now he saw there were sharp teeth lining its jaws. The buck lowered his head for a charge that would drive its sharp antlers right through Ti Frere and into the big tree.

Ti Frere struggled to wake up. He closed and opened his eyes over and over but each time, the scene remained unchanged, and the dark wind continued to moan through the trees, louder and louder. Ti Frere swung his head from side to side: "Why me?" he screamed. "What did I do?" Then he saw his grandfather standing on the little island to his left, glowing in the same way as the other creatures. "Vieux Pop!" Ti Frere called out, but when the boy tried to run to his grandfather, he stumbled and fell. He struggled to his feet and looked up, but the old man was gone. He turned quickly to face the attacking spirits, if that is what they were, but they too were gone. There was only a bass in the water near his pirogue, a beautiful buck walking into the trees only fifty feet away, and Ti Bird circling above and calling, his wings catching the first golden rays of the rising sun. Ti Frere walked to the place where he had seen Vieux Pop standing, but the ground was covered with cypress needles and he couldn't find any footprints. He stepped to the water's edge and squatted there, splashing water into his eyes and face, trying to determine whether the dream was over, or whether it had been a dream at all.

The sky was clear, and a low fog clung to the surface of the water. As Ti Frere dried his eyes on his shirt sleeve, he turned and looked out toward the west. There he saw the passageway that Vieux Pop had described, the tunnel-like path that had been made when the huge logs were dragged through the swamp more than sixty years earlier.

In the light of early morning, Ti Frere turned to look at the giant tree, now that he could see it well. He ran his fingers over the bark in the area where a door had opened for him during the night. Entering the tree had been a dream, but it seemed as real to him now as any event in his life, and the glowing spirits, strange as they were, seemed even more real than other things, though he could not begin to understand what their meaning might possibly be. He could close his eyes and see everything in his mind as it had been during the night, and he found it difficult to push the images aside and enter the day that was progressing around him. He walked all the way around the big tree once more and looked up at its towering trunk. From the branches just above his head, a young raccoon looked back at him.

A barred owl, made uneasy by Ti Frere's gaze, turned its head nervously before flying off to a nearby tree. A pair of fox squirrels chattered happily and chased each other from branch to branch a hundred feet above the boy. Finally, when Ti Frere had satisfied himself that the tree was as real as he was, he walked slowly to his pirogue. Moccasin had already settled himself comfortably in the middle of the boat, and Ti Bird was perched on the bow, ready to continue the journey through this new territory.

Confused by the events of the night and weakened from lack of food, Ti Frere had already started paddling toward the tunnel-like passageway leading away from the tree when he remembered to look for the axehead stuck into the stump where Wilson had sat on the day the big tree's life was spared. He turned around, looked back and saw three objects more clearly than anything else in the vast swamp: the huge tree against whose trunk he had slept, an enormous stump about forty feet to the left—*that must have been Mr. Choupique's 1,869-year-old record holder*—and another big stump to the right where Wilson had probably sat smoking, waiting for his reluctant crew to saw down the last big tree.

The axe bit was still protruding from this stump, though some of the sapwood had rotted away, exposing more of the bit than had shown on the day it had become imbedded. The boy thought of removing the now rusty piece of metal and taking it home with him, but he felt he should leave it where it had remained these many years. Ti Frere paddled to the bigger of the two stumps and stepped out of his pirogue into the shallow water. Placing a bare foot into an old springboard hole, he lifted himself to the flat top of the stump. The annual rings stood out now as hundreds of tiny ridges, the softer wood between them having finally begun to decay. Ti Frere put his right index finger at the exact center of what had been the old tree's heart. "71 A.D.," he said aloud.

Then he lay with his back against the stump and looked up at the morning sky. Another flock of geese was passing high overhead, and he began counting them. "Migration is a mystery," Vieux Pop had said. Ti Frere could remember just when he had said it. They were sitting around the woodstove a week before Christmas last year, and Aristile was putting an edge on his old bone-handled skinning knife that he had sharpened so many times for so many years that it was more handle than blade now. A late-migrating flock of geese had gone by, and Aristile had stopped to listen. "Don't lose sight of anything in life that is a mystery," he had said. "Well, Vieux Pop, it's a mystery to me how you could cut all those trees and never tell me about it," the boy thought. "I'm not losing sight of that; you can count on it."

Ti Frere watched until the last of the geese were gone; then he climbed down to the water. His muscles were sore and knotted as he paddled his big pirogue into the passageway that Vieux Pop had told him would lead straight to Six Hundred Dollar Bayou. He knew that the trip would not be an easy one.

I haven't eaten anything since that supper on the porch—when was it?—day before yesterday, I guess. Seems longer than that. I'm cold and damp. I didn't sleep well, even though I was surely tired enough. I'm only beginning to find my way out now and I'm already exhausted. For all its safety, I wish my pirogue were smaller and lighter. I don't know if I can make it all the way out to the bayou.

Cottonmouth

Ti Frere had gone only about two miles when he thought he could see the big oaks that Vieux Pop had described, the ones where Indians had once lived. He became excited by the prospect of being almost halfway out and he began paddling faster and less cautiously. He realized his mistake only after his heavy pirogue had slid up on a slightly submerged cypress log and stuck there. There are times when a boat lodged on a log or stump can be moved off by simply shifting the weight in the boat away from the point that is in contact with the submerged object. But sometimes the boat is so solidly stuck that it won't float off, and one must get into the water to pull it free.

Ti Frere put a hand on each side of him, planning to raise himself, as he always did, from a sitting to a standing position, by using the pirogue's gunwales as supports. Then he saw that only three inches from where his right hand lay was a thick-bodied cottonmouth moccasin, coiled and motionless on a little branch that protruded from the submerged log. Ti Frere froze, knowing that if he pulled his hand away suddenly the big snake would strike. Weak and exhausted as he was, and hot from paddling as fast as he could, the boy knew that the poison would course quickly through his blood, and that he would not likely survive.

"It's too late for them to be out," Ti Frere thought as new beads of sweat began to form on his skin. "Snakes should be hibernating in late November. It's not right." The boy sat more still than he ever had at any time in his short life. "You can smell a moccasin before you see him, if you keep your nose turned on," Vieux Pop had told him. His eyes met the hooded eyes of the serpent, and he watched the reptile's tongue slithering in and out of its mouth. "A cottonmouth can taste the air with his tongue. He can sense if you're hostile or not." Every detail of the big snake's flat wedge-like head and heavy jaws was clear and sharp to him. Its eyes seemed the essence of evil, though the boy knew that no wild creature is either good or evil. Ti Bird had flown off when the pirogue hit the log, and Moccasin watched the snake, not knowing whether to attack or wait, having received no sign from Ti Frere. The tension was almost deafening, and the moment seemed endless. Finally, when Ti Frere was about to try to move his hand slowly back and away, the cottonmouth shifted its eyes to look at Moccasin, who had begun to growl deep in his throat; then it began very slowly to uncoil its heavy body and back down into the water, choosing to spare the now trembling boy.

For several minutes Ti Frere sat motionless, relieved and drained. When he had recovered, he moved to the rear of his pirogue and called Moccasin to him. With their combined weight away from the pirogue's point of lodging, Ti Frere was able to push the boat backward off the log, go around it, and continue his journey.

The oaks Ti Frere had seen before his encounter with the cotton-mouth were not the ones Vieux Pop had told him about, and he began to fear that he was lost again, but he kept on paddling. It was another two miles before he saw the big evergreens standing in the water on both sides of his passageway. He felt encouraged and strengthened by the certainty that he was close to finding his way out of Buffalo Swamp, and that he was finished with being lost. Ti Frere paddled his pirogue through the roots and directly beneath the immense trunk of the largest of the strange oaks. Moccasin growled a warning at whatever creature he imagined might be hiding in the darkness among the roots that formed a ceiling above them. Ti Bird had flown from his favorite perch and landed in the branches of the big oak before the pirogue entered the root system. The boy stopped under the tree, fascinated by a thing he had never before experienced, to be below the trunk of a living tree; but Ti Bird became concerned when the expected exit of the pirogue didn't occur, and he began calling worriedly for his friends.

Ti Frere sat quietly for a while, trying to imagine what the lives of the Indians might have been like. He knew that the Chitimacha had lived here and elsewhere in the Basin for hundreds of years before the white people came. He knew that they were even closer to nature and wildlife than he and his grandfather were, and that they had not destroyed the cypress forest as the white people had, but he knew nothing of their day-to-day lives: what they ate, how they hunted, whether they lived peacefully, how they survived the mosquitos in summer and the cold in winter.

I read a little about the Chitimacha people in the library at school. One book said that the tribe had gotten into a terrible war with the French in the early 1700s, and was nearly wiped out. That was before the Cajuns came here. I asked my teacher for some more information, but she didn't know anything, so I dropped it. I'll have to ask Vieux Pop. He told me one time that he had known some of the Indians before they all moved away. I don't even know where they went, and I don't know why they left the Basin. He said they were closer to the spirits than we are.

Ti Frere picked up his paddle, patted Moccasin on the head and called to Ti Bird as he maneuvered his pirogue through the big oak's massive roots and back into the straight-cut passsageway out to Six Hundred Dollar Bayou. He pushed on with a strength built of optimism, hope and a growing desire to be reconciled with Vieux Pop. He knew his dark journey into the depths of Buffalo Swamp was nearing its end.

I always know when Vieux Pop has something important to say to me. "Come on, Ti Frere, let's go take a walk," he'll say, and we'll start off down one of the several trails that go off into the woods behind the back fence of our yard. Some days we talk about patience; sometimes, open-mindedness. He often talks about determination. He has more ideas than all the teachers at my school put together. I wonder what it was that kept him from telling me anything about his logging days.

I guess I'm beginning to feel a little better about Vieux Pop. I hope he'll be at the bayou waiting for me, but he might not. He never knew what direction I went when I left the house. He wasn't even there.

He must have had a reason to cut the big trees. He's the best person I know, and if he did something wrong, there has to be a reason. I guess I never gave him a good chance to explain before I got mad and ran away from him. Now I miss seeing his face and hearing his voice. I guess I made him sad.

Reunion

Vieux Pop was waiting at the bayou and Ti Frere knew as he approached that the old man had been there for a long time, for Aristile's putt-putt motor could have been heard for miles across the quiet swamp, and Ti Frere had not heard it: "I wonder if Vieux Pop spent the night here on the bayou waiting for me," he thought. "How did he know that I'd come out here?" When his pirogue slid up on the bank next to the old man's boat, Ti Frere jumped up and began running toward his grandfather, almost stumbling over Moccasin, who was barking excitedly and dancing all around Vieux Pop. The young boy bumped into the old man and hugged him tightly, almost knocking him off his feet. Then he stood back and they both laughed, before either spoke a word. "I'm sorry, Vieux Pop," Ti Frere said, just as Vieux Pop said, *"Toe doit gan fain."* (You must be hungry). Then Aristile said, "We miss' you, boy," just as Ti Frere said, *"Ma pay mort de fain."* (I'm dying of hunger). Then they laughed again at the confusion of speaking at the same time and in different languages.

Finally, they got into Vieux Pop's boat, where Ti Frere changed into dry clothes and Aristile began laying out the food he had brought: roast venison sandwiches on Octavie's homemade bread, cold sweet potatoes and cornbread with cheese baked inside it. Then he pulled up from the water a quart-sized bottle of fresh milk that he had earlier lowered on a long string into the cold depths of the bayou. Ti Frere devoured one of the sandwiches as Vieux Pop threw meat scraps to Moccasin and then fed Ti Bird, holding bits of fish in his lightly closed fist, making the young hawk probe with his beak to find them. It was a game the old man had often seen his grandson play with Ti Bird.

Ti Frere had nearly finished his second sandwich and Vieux Pop was making some minor adjustments on his putt-putt motor when Aristile decided that there would be no better time to try to explain to Alexson what had happened when he had accepted work as a logger. He reached over and touched his grandson to get his attention: "Ti Frere," he began, "as a cutter of big trees I was very good—a champion. I was nearly as good with an axe as Lash Larue was with his long whip. I could drop a big tree and before it hit the ground, my sharp axe was biting into the next tree. I had jumped from one springboard to the next. We must do what we can do best in this life. Pride in cutting trees was one of my vines. I could have done something else...I know that now, but at that time, there was no one to uproot that vine and pull it off of me. Anyhow, I would not have let it happen. Not even Choupique could help me. I was twenty years old!

"I could have made boats, I could have made nets and caught fish and turtles as I do now. But cutting trees was what I wanted to do, and I was well paid by the land company. I thought I was something special. I didn't let myself feel anything for the great forest I was helping to destroy. All I could see were the trees that waited to be cut. I had no more understanding of what I was doing than a hound dog understands the deer he chases, so that the hunter can shoot it. If the dog does his work right, he is petted, praised and fed well. What does he care about the deer? If there comes a time when all the deer are killed, the dog will have to be trained to do something else. What about the people who wanted only to see the deer and to live in a world where deer could walk safely through ancient forests? As far as the dog is concerned, or the hunters, let those people visit the zoo."

Aristile filled his fuel tank from an old five-gallon can of gasoline he always kept under a canvas tarpaulin at the back of the boat. He looked at Ti Frere, who was settling himself and Moccasin on a pile of old sacks toward the middle of the boat. He knew that the boy would soon be asleep, in spite of the loudness of the putt-putt engine.

"Do you pity the deer, Ti Frere, and the enchanted forest that has been converted into cutover swampland? Then pity me also," the old fisherman said, as he reached over and put his hand on the sleepy boy's shoulder. "I am a man who destroyed, with my own hands, the greatest and most beautiful thing I have ever seen with my own eyes."

"Vieux Pop," the boy said, with his head lowered. Then he looked straight into Aristile's grey eyes: "I shot a rabbit. And I threw it into the water."

"I know. I saw it."

"I'm sorry."

"I know."

Aristile settled back into his old cypress boat seat, worn smooth and shiny by many years of contact with the seat of his pants; he gave the flywheel a spin, and his old putt-putt engine popped loudly to life.

Alexson was already asleep by the time Aristile had guided the boat, with pirogue in tow, away from the bank and into the middle of the bayou.

"Listen, Ti Frere," he said; he reached toward his grandson, then realized that the boy was sleeping. Aristile spoke anyway, not to himself exactly, but almost inaudibly, against a cold late November wind and the noise of the simple old engine: "I wanted to tell you, Alexson, that I think I have begun to understand the poster that hangs on my wall. I believe that people's greatest challenge may be to discover the meekness that is our true nature." He paused.

"We'll find time to talk about it one day, maybe tomorrow." He paused again.

"Well, maybe next year."

Epilogue

For Vieux Pop the Atchafalaya Basin was the center of the universe. He sometimes called the river "de almighty." He communicated with the spirits in nature. His presence will never leave the big woods. I can feel it there every time I go back, and I wonder why I left. Where's the center of the universe for me, for Ti Frere? I've banged around north and south, east and west, and I'm still searching for something, like Wilferd in the old chest, and I hear someone laughing.

The Basin is the only place that provides me peace of mind. If I close my eyes, I can see Vieux Pop building a pirogue, and tracking a deer through the dry November woods. I can see him stirring gumbo at the big woodstove, playing cards and making music with his friends. Every detail is clear and sharp, like images in an old black and white photograph. And I'm still sitting there on the woodbox, half-asleep, dreaming of the giant trees that will never be again.

I can hear music from his accordion and the loud noise of his two-cylinder putt-putt motor boat echoing through the swamps. I can smell the coffee and the gumbo heating on the woodstove. I believe that the center of my universe lies in the memory of Vieux Pop, and in understanding the meaning of his life, for I suspect that I am not yet unlost.

c'est tout
The End

Any fool can destroy trees. They
cannot run away; and if they could...
they would be...hunted down as long
as fun or a dollar could be got out
of their bark hides...Through all
the wonderful, eventful centuries
since Christ's time—and long before
that—God has cared for these trees...
but he cannot save them from fools—
only Uncle Sam can do that.

John Muir
1838 - 1914

Sealth Speaks:

The earth is our mother. Let us start with that.

How can one buy or sell the air, the warmth of the land? That is
difficult for us to imagine. We do not own the sweet air or the sparkle on
the water. How then can you buy them from us?

Each pine tree shining in the sun, each sandy beach, the mist
hanging in the dark woods, every space, each humming bee, every part of
the earth is sacred to my people, holy in their memory and experience.

We are part of the earth and the earth is part of us. The fragrant
flowers are our sisters. The reindeer, the horse, the great eagle are our
brothers. The rocky heights, the foamy crests of waves in the river, the sap
of meadow flowers, the body heat of the pony—and of human beings—all

belong to the same family.

So when the Great Chief in Washington sends word that he wants to buy our land, he asks a great deal of us.

We know that the white man does not understand our way of life. To him, one piece of land is much like another. He is a stranger who comes in the night and takes from the land whatever he needs. The earth is not his friend but his enemy, and when he has conquered it, he moves on. He cares nothing for the land. He forgets his parents' graves and his children's heritage. He kidnaps the earth from his children. He treats his mother the earth and his brother the sky like merchandise. His hunger will eat the earth bare and leave only a desert.

I have seen a thousand buffalo left behind by the White Man—shot from a passing train. I am a savage and cannot understand why the puffing iron horse should be more important than the buffalo, which we kill only in order to stay alive. What are human beings without animals? If all the animals ceased to exist, human beings would die of a great loneliness of the spirit. For whatever happens to the animals, will happen soon also to human beings. Continue to soil your bed and one night you will suffocate in your own waste.

Humankind has not woven the web of life. We are but one thread within it. Whatever we do to the web we do to ourselves. All things are bound together. All things connect. Whatever befalls the earth befalls also the children of the earth.

—Sealth (known to whites as Chief Seattle)
Address to President Franklin Pierce – 1855

Greg Guirard   (318) 394-4631
1470 Bayou Mercier Road
St. Martinville, LA 70582